CROSSING A COYOTE

"Do you remember a kid named Julio, Duke? This one was a kid from down south. Julio Cervantes. He paid you to bring him across one night. He never made it to the other side, and he never made it back south either.

Braxton shrugged. "Who remembers? Something happens, the Mexes all split, who the hell knows what might happen to them afterward. I can't be responsible for all of them, man. You ought to know that. Besides, what do you care? It's no fat off your ox."

"Fact is, Duke, it is my affair." I smiled at him. "I was hired to come down here and take it real personal about Julio."

The talk was just so much cover-up, trying to take my attention off what he was doing and put it onto what he was saying.

His hand moved, and he snatched at the gun behind his belt.

I whapped him with the bag of money. Kinda like a little old lady swatting a mugger with her purse.

The burlap connected with the automatic Braxton was pulling, and the thing went flying.

Christians 1, Lions 0.

Instead of running, he came at me. Fast.

Other Carl Heller novels by Frank Roderus
Ask your bookseller for the books you have missed

THE OIL RIG
THE RAIN RUSTLERS
THE VIDEO VANDAL
THE TURN-OUT MAN

A HELLER NOVEL

THE COYOTE CROSSING

Frank Roderus

BANTAM BOOKS
TORONTO • NEW YORK • LONDON • SYDNEY • AUCKLAND

THE COYOTE CROSSING

A Bantam Book / April 1985

ISBN 0-553-24706-9

Published simultaneously in the United States and Canada

Bantam Books are published by Bantam Books, Inc. Its trademark, consisting of the words "Bantam Books" and the portrayal of a rooster, is Registered in U.S. Patent and Trademark Office and in other countries. Marca Registrada. Bantam Books, Inc., 666 Fifth Avenue, New York, New York 10103.

PRINTED IN THE UNITED STATES OF AMERICA

O 0 9 8 7 6 5 4 3 2 1

For Ed and Joanne Sherman

THE COYOTE CROSSING

1

The judges were breaking my heart, I tell you. It was awful.

Here I was at the first NCHA-approved cutting that had been held anywhere within a single day's hauling distance for the past two months, the only dang one that would be held close to home for several more months to come, and where the devil was I? Sitting on a damn arena rail, that's where.

All around me was the smell of tobacco and horse sweat and hoof-churned tanbark. Horses stood tied all around the steel-pipe walls of the arena, and the back end of the working area, behind the judges' elevated plywood towers, was full of stamping, milling, waiting horses and men. Most sat and watched, and a few, who would be up soon, were cantering in tight little figure-8s to get their animals warmed up and ready.

Me, I was sitting there thinking how very well my good filly would have done, *should* have done, the way the judging was going in Non-Pro Novice.

This would have been the first competition for her, after all the hours and months of training that filly and I had put in together.

And she was ready for it. Would have been ready for it. The youngun had so much plain, raw, natural talent that even my fumbling couldn't have discouraged her from the business of dominating bovines.

Out in the business end of the arena, Billy Kester rode forward on a tough-looking, short-coupled gray colt that was running sweat from a combination of nervousness and warmup exercises. The timer gave him the signal to start his two and a half minutes of work, and Billy bumped the gray into the contrary mass of whiteface calves.

It looked like Billy wanted to take one out of the middle, but the gray braced its forelegs and shook its head a little. Balking already, I thought with an unkind flush of self-satisfied superiority. Instead of insisting on the calf he wanted, Billy took the easy way out and peeled one off the outside of the herd. The calf he drove out was smallish and had a slightly pale coat with a brown manure stain on its near hip. I'd seen that particular calf worked twice before already and knew Billy had made a bad choice.

The gray pushed the calf out from the herd, and the turnback men drifted into position to make it try a run back into the security of the little herd of fourteen other calves. The object of the whole competition was to see just how well the cutting horse could hold the calf out where it didn't want to be, to see just how well and how stylishly the horse could impose its will on the six-hundred-pound bovine.

Not too darn well in this case.

Billy's gray set itself all right, head to head with the calf, rump toward the herd that was milling in a corner of the arena, body angled slightly into the center of the working area in anticipation of a run across the arena. The horse stood low in the front end, ears forward and head low, forelegs poised for a cat-quick response to the calf's breakaway movement. Seven times out of ten the gray would have been holding himself just right for the break.

But like I said, I'd seen this calf work already, and it was pretty much of an idjit.

Instead of wheeling out toward the center of the arena, the calf let its head sag and gave out a bawl. It didn't *like* being out here by its lonesome, and those turnback riders on their big horses were crowding it from behind.

The calf tossed its head, throwing strings of snot, and made a dive toward the fence. Almost straight for the gray's head. It was kinda like Robert Newhouse bucking the Orange Crush. Pick a direction and go like hell.

The gray was confused. It tried to spin back over its hocks and slam the wall before the calf could get there, but it was just too late. It bumped the calf with its shoulder, and several hundred pounds of frightened meat bounced off the rails with a squeal and a dull thump. Then the calf was back into the protection of the herd, and Billy was sitting there with egg on his face.

The competition was already blown for him, but he went through the motions of it anyway, doing a fairly creditable job with his next calf but working it too long, so that he was back in the herd again hunting a third one to work when the whistle blew and his time was over. He was shaking his head when he rode off the floor.

And at that, darn it, they scored him a seventy.

It just wouldn't have been human not to make a comparison with what my own good filly could have done.

If she'd been there.

Instead she was back home at the ranch north of Lake George, wandering happily from the hay bunk to the water tank and back again. Limping on a muscle pull in the left hind. Dammit. She had been so ready, and then that had happened. At least, I reminded myself, she wasn't injured either permanently or seriously. Given a little time, she would be just fine again.

Meanwhile, I was having to watch other fellows go out there and have their fun.

I sighed some and tugged my hat down a little lower over my eyes. If nothing else, I was enjoying the company. There aren't so many cuttings held around close to home that a person could get tired of seeing the same faces all the time. It was a treat when the opportunities did arise.

Roy Fisk came up behind me in the alleyway on one of those stout young paint studs that he always seems to have in his barn. I've never been all that high on loud-colored horses, but there are people in the business these days who are breeding some awfully well-built animals underneath those crazy coats, and Roy knows how to make them work. I made some admiring noises without having to lie about a thing, and we chatted for a while about his family and the prospects he was training. After a few minutes he glanced off behind me somewhere and said, "Looks like somebody wants to see you, Carl." He grinned. "Better luck next time." Naturally I'd had to tell him my tale of woe about the filly. He touched the brim of his seminew, almost-clean show hat—you should see the one he wears around the barn at home—and moved off on the big black-and-white paint. I turned to see what he was talking about.

There was a woman there, giving me a tentative, mostly embarrassed sort of half-smile. I didn't recognize her.

I guessed her at fortyish, with coarse, dark hair going to silvery gray and worn very short. She had on the kind of jeans that I knew without her having to turn around would carry some fashion designer's label over a back pocket, loafers instead of boots, and a blue and white pullover shirt. She looked kind of out-of-place here. There are practically no spectators at a cutting contest, and while I don't know all the wives and daughters—and women competitors—I've probably seen most of them often enough over the years to recognize them as belonging to the group. This woman I was pretty sure I hadn't seen before.

She looked at me like she knew me, though, although there was nothing about me that would make me stand out from this crowd. Stetson on top and Justins underneath. In between there was a pretty fit 180 pounds stretched over something just short of the macho-image six feet. Dark blond hair that could have been cut more recently than it had been. Features okay but hardly the sort of thing to make a stranger's heart pound. Probably thirty percent of the male humans on the grounds here would have fit the same description. And certainly ninety percent of the horses were more worthy of being looked at.

Yet, when the eye contact was made and she realized that Roy had given her an opportunity for conversation, her smile firmed a little and she walked toward me.

"Hello, Carl." No question mark in that tone of voice. Still a little tentative, though. "It's been a long time."

I pushed a smile out in front of the puzzlement I was feeling and swung around to drop down off the railing to ground level. Standing in front of her, I found she was a tad taller than most. Call it five-seven or close to that. It gave me no clues, and I wasn't sure what to say next. Obviously I was supposed to know her. I didn't. Her eyes were a soft, luminous, golden brown. Glistening now with moisture. That didn't help a bit.

The already-uncertain smile of greeting wavered, then steadied as if by an effort of will. "You don't recognize me."

"I'm sorry."

"It *has* been a long time." She pushed a hand forward. Long, impeccably groomed scarlet nails contrasting with dry, aged-looking skin. Her smile looked phony now, and there was more moisture welling up beneath her eyes. "It's Leah, Carl. Leah Crowder."

I felt like she had just hit me, and I probably looked like an ass standing there with the handshake forgotten and unreleased, gaping at her. For sure I felt like one.

Once upon a time, not so very long ago, I had been close enough to Leah Crowder to give *very* serious consideration to marriage. It had been that kind of relationship. Very intense. Now I stood there staring at her, and, heaven help me, I swear to God I still couldn't recognize Leah in this woman who was standing in front of me.

2

"It has been . . . illuminating," Leah said softly. "I couldn't claim that it has been worthwhile, particularly, but it certainly has been instructive." She swirled the thin stick of white plastic through her nondairy-creamed coffee.

We were huddled across from each other in a booth at McDonald's. I'd thought it was the closest place where we could find some privacy and a cup of coffee. I'd been wrong about that. The coffee was fine, but on a weekend the mid-morning hour was no inducement for privacy. Hyperactive children and weary parents and scruffy teenagers roamed past incessantly, and the noise level was far above what this conversation called for.

"Are you coping with it?"

She gave me another smile, a very genuine one this time. "Thank you."

"For what?"

"For not offering platitudes. You know. 'Everything is going to be all right.' 'They're learning more about it all the time.' All the crap that people say when they don't know what to say."

Well, I didn't exactly know what to say either, so I kept my mouth shut and took a short, slurping sip of the too-hot coffee.

"I didn't answer your question, did I?" Leah sighed. "I don't know that I've learned to cope, exactly, but I can more or less accept it at this point. I still get angry sometimes, but I've gotten pretty much through the why-me-woe-is-me stage. I mean, I don't *want* to die, particularly. But I've accepted the reality that I'm going to." No smile this time. A great deal of intensity. Leah had always been a very intense human being, I remembered.

Apparently she still was.

Cancer, she said it was. The ugliest of all possible words today. Cancers, she had elaborated. Plural form. Breast, lymph, uterine, now colon.

"I'm a teaching hospital's dream come true," she said with false levity. "They snip here and they snip there. I'm better than any chart for showing postsurgical residues."

"Don't."

"It's all right, Carl. Really. I'm not truly bitter. Just a little angry now and then."

I nodded. "What about Mac?"

Mac was, or had been, L. Ron MacPherson. Very solid citizen. Very steady and secure in his slow, upward mobility. I'd always thought the man a bit of a prick, but then my judgment was admittedly clouded on that subject. After Leah and I had decided—hell, admit it, Carl, after Leah had decided—that physical intensity is not sufficient grounds to commit marriage, she had turned to Mac for permanence. The last I knew she had been Mrs. L. Ron etc. Now she seemed to be using the maiden name again.

"It isn't just people who get cancer, Carl. Families do. The difference is that Mac was given more choices than I was. He was just fine through the hysterectomy and the cervical thing. We hadn't really wanted children anyway."

That one struck me as odd. Leah had definitely wanted kids back in the used-to times that I could remember. She'd never talked about it at the time, but I'd always been convinced that my erratic lifestyle made me suspect in her mind as a potential papa.

"He really did try, Carl. It was the mastectomy that was too much for him. Too much of a gross-out getting into bed with a woman with one tit and a bunch of scar tissue where the other one ought to be.

"Then there was the chemotherapy, of course." She grinned. "Sorry. It's a very serious subject, but every time I say the word *chemotherapy* out loud I think of the Lone Ranger and Tonto. You know. Kemo sabe. Kemo therapy. Anyway, that was a gross-out too. All the hair comes out. I mean *all* of it." She touched the short, coarse, graying mop of hair on her head. "This is what came back up top. You don't want to see what came back elsewhere. Not that Mac hung around that long."

I looked at the dark hair with its slightly silvery sheen, and if I hadn't known Leah so very well before, I would have found it attractive enough. It was the contrast that was unnerving.

Leah was—I tried to remember—still in her twenties, even though I had taken her for forty or so when I had seen her back at the arena. I could remember her birthdate—July 12. I just wasn't sure of the year. She would be, I thought, twenty-seven or twenty-eight now.

When I had known her before she had been a big, healthy, very full-bodied gal. A rock scrambler and tennis player with all the physical equipment for hard play. And vigorous loving. She'd had chestnut-colored hair, and a lot of it. And her breasts—how many times had I touched them and enjoyed them and pillowed myself against them—had been in proportion with that fine, full body.

I still couldn't believe the differences between that woman and this one.

With a bit of a shock I realized that I was honestly thinking of her in terms of being two separate women, then and now.

Jesus, how unfair can you be to someone you like?

"By that time," she was saying, "Mac had already had more than enough. Not that I blame him. The poor guy was just plain turned off by this gross thing he was supposed to sleep with. I guess it was a blessing in disguise that one of the side effects of the chemo was, for me anyway, a complete loss of interest in sex." She smiled. "If you can believe that. It's true, anyway."

Leah had always been every bit as intense in bed as on the tennis court. I could remember that with no prompting whatsoever. Her eagerness had quickly become a very fondly recurring joke between us back then.

"I have to give Mac credit for the way he handled it," she said. "He thought it over, and when he was sure he came to me and sat me down on the couch and told me straight out. It was a rather stuffy lecture, about a man's needs and all that. But then Mac was a rather stuffy man. And he told me what he had decided *before* he went and found someone to replace me in the king-sized bed." The tears wanted to flow. I could see them lying there. But she wasn't going to let them out. She fought them back somehow. "I rather admire him for that," she said.

I grunted. Which was *much* more polite than saying what I really wanted to say.

"We came to terms on a settlement." She snorted, and this time I thought she did sound fairly bitter. "By then they had found more tumors, so we both knew I wouldn't need very much. And Mac agreed to provide me with medical-insurance coverage through the firm."

I didn't ask what firm. By now the son of a bitch probably had his own. The hell with him. I really didn't want to discuss the man's successes when I was sitting with clear evidence of his failures.

"So," Leah said, "I'm really a lot better off than most people in my position. And I guess that in most of the ways that count I am coping. Or learning to." She took a deep breath. "I don't have a lot of time, Carl, and there are some things that I need to take care of while I still can."

Leah looked very nervous again. As uncertain as she had looked back at the arena.

"Is there anything I can do?" I had the impression that there would be. Leah Crowder had not had the kind of interests that would have brought her on her own to a cutting contest, and I seriously doubted that marriage to a prig like L. Ron MacPherson would have generated new interests in that direction.

"There is something," she said, "but only if you promise

me you'll think about it as a business proposition, not as some kind of sympathy ploy from an old girl friend. I didn't tell you all this for that, Carl." She looked at me with such earnestness that I had to believe her, and I told her so. "I told you because it is necessary to the arrangement I'm going to propose."

"All right."

Leah took another deep breath and began talking again.

3

What it came down to was something very simple, very basic. She had a matter of months left. One, two, probably no more than six. Leah was a tidy person. She wanted to be able to die knowing that all her obligations had been met, all her debts paid. Not just the financial obligations; she had already taken care of those with the help of an estate lawyer. Now she was trying to clear a moral debt. She wondered if I was still so . . . indignant.

"I still have the same quirks, Leah." I smiled at her. "To put it in terms that you might remember—no, I've haven't grown up or settled down yet."

She winced a little. Apparently Leah remembered that last conversation we had had. Certainly I could still recall it, all too well. "Twisting an old knife, Carl?"

"I didn't mean to."

A bit of smile tickled the corners of a mouth that was a little too wide and full and fresh for the age that had crept into the rest of her once-lovely face. "No false sympathies here," she said. "That's awfully refreshing, you know." I got the impression she wanted to reach over and touch my hand, but she didn't. She seemed to be holding herself in check against something. Pain, I guessed. It must be pretty constant at this point. "I'm glad you haven't changed, Carl. I never thought I would *ever* say this, but I think the peculiar way you are bent could be a big comfort to me now."

That was almost as much of a surprise to me as her cancer had been. Once upon a time, Leah Crowder had scoured deep into the reasons behind my odd lifestyle, thought them over with great care, and concluded finally that she could not permanently approve of a man with such an abnormal view of authority and social order. She had wondered if I could change. For her. I'd thought that question over just as carefully and told her as honestly as I could that I probably couldn't. Neither of us had realized it at the time, but our relationship had effectively ended there and then.

Oh, we'd struggled on for a few months more, but both of us should have been brighter than that. We hadn't been. The last conversation had included undertones of anger that had made both of us do some sniping and knife twisting.

And since then, no, I hadn't really changed all that much.

Once upon a time, back before Leah, I had come to the conclusion that right and wrong have very little, remarkably little, to do with what is legal or illegal. Law and justice just aren't the same concepts. They are related only on the surface, only in appearance. Down in the guts of the matter, where it counts, they are wholly separate ideals.

It hurt, learning that. I had to do a lot of soul-searching

about it. When I was done, I couldn't help but discover that I cared more about justice than I did about law.

Since then I've been called a vigilante by more than one person. Leah had used the term herself, if I remember correctly. And I was awfully sure that I did.

I don't really think the word applies. Abuse in the form of early-day terrorism has given the word *vigilante* a distinctly negative connotation. It is that, I think, and not the concept itself that offends me about the term.

Whatever you want to call it, though, the fact remains. There are times when duly constituted law cannot or more often *will* not make any attempt to do right by people. That offends me. When I find out about it I get kind of, as Leah put it, indignant. I want to make things right.

Sometimes I can.

And I'm not so proud that I won't take a financial gift as a way of saying thank you when I've been able to help someone.

That isn't just greed, I like to keep telling myself. The ranch, the few head of horses, and a few more of registered Longhorn cattle, bring in enough to pay the taxes and keep me in beans. It is the occasional chunk of extra money that gives me the freedom to go out and raise hell when I find something to be indignant about.

I sighed. Leah knew all about this. Not many people do, but it isn't the sort of thing a man keeps from a woman he is thinking of sharing the rest of his life with. So we had talked about it at length back then, once upon a time, and she had not approved.

Now she seemed to have gotten a different perspective on it, or at least had decided it was less bad than whatever it was that was bothering her.

I sat back and listened to her explain.

The girl's name was Estella Maria something-or-other Cervantes. For more than a year and a half, since before Mac had moved out, she had been living with Leah. She was maid, nurse, cook, companion, and, I gathered, most important, for all the ugly months someone who would be there day or night, someone Leah could hold on to and cry with when the pain and the hopelessness were at their worst. For more than a year this girl had been the only *good* constant in Leah's life. Leah felt she owed this girl more than any financial settlement could ever repay.

"She is . . . undocumented, Carl. An illegal alien. A 'wet' if you prefer."

She paused for a moment, and I wondered if she was waiting for some reaction of shock or disapproval. Probably, I thought. Hiring an illegal alien was probably illegal also—I was a bit fuzzy on that point, probably because I didn't particularly care—and Leah had always had a very rigid and straitlaced view of the law.

"I didn't know she was undocumented when Mac hired her. I don't honestly know if Mac was aware of it or not. By the time I did realize it I, well, I just couldn't turn her away. She meant too much to me by then. And it would have been cruel. She wasn't paid slave wages or anything like that either, Carl. Please understand that."

"That never would have crossed my mind, Leah."

She smiled. "I guess not." She sighed. "Stella is a wonderful person, Carl. A dear, dear friend. And right now there is a horrid burden on her. On her whole family."

"She has family here?"

Leah shook her head. "In Zacatecas."

I raised my eyebrows.

"I'm sorry. Back home in Mexico. Zacatecas is the state.

There's a city by that name also. Stella comes from Nieves, if it makes any differences."

"Oh." I had never heard of either.

"It isn't a very prosperous area, and with their economy being what it is. . . ." Leah spread her hands and shrugged. It was enough.

"She sends as much home as she can, but it hasn't been enough. A few months ago her brother wrote saying he was going to come north to work too." Leah looked embarrassed. When she went on I understood why. "Stella and I talked it over. We thought if he came here to join her he could live at the house—there's an awful lot of room in it, you see—and find a job up here. Stella . . ." another sigh, "*we* sent him money for the trip. Enough to get to the border—Nieves isn't far off the highway north through Juárez—and to hire a coyote to get him across and then take a bus to Pueblo. We were to meet him there. There are plenty of Hispanics in Pueblo, of course, and it's an easy drive from home. Oh, I guess you wouldn't know. My house, it was part of the settlement with Mac, is near Cotopaxi."

I know the area. It's a small community on the Arkansas River west of Canon City and the Royal Gorge. Not terribly far from my place by the country roads. Leah had been living that close, and in trouble, and I hadn't known it.

"Anyway, Carl, we had it all arranged. Or thought we did. Julio had the telephone number and the bus schedules, and he said he had a friend who could put him in contact with a coyote. That's what they call a person who arranges border crossings for a fee."

That much I had heard before.

"It's supposed to be much safer than trying to cross alone, because the coyote will also arrange transportation away from the border, away from the Border Patrol. Some of them arrange jobs too, all over the country. It . . . isn't legal, of course."

That was the sort of thing that Leah would find very difficult to admit, so I tried to give no reaction.

"We know Julio left home when he planned, and he spent two nights with a relative in Juárez. Apparently he had everything arranged with the coyote. He was supposed to cross two weeks ago." There was a pain in Leah's eyes that had nothing to do with anything physically wrong with her. "He hasn't been heard from since."

"That must be pretty tough on Stella."

She nodded, and the pain she was feeling was very obvious.

"You're feeling guilty about it, aren't you, Leah?"

"I helped arrange it, Carl. I sent the boy the money for him to come here. I thought I was *helping*. I wouldn't . . . couldn't do anything to hurt Stella like this."

It was my turn to sigh.

"Stella, we, both of us are afraid something happened to him. Her whole family is petrified, Carl. They want to know what has happened to him. If nothing else, well, just being able to have a Mass said for him would help ease their suffering. If that's all they can still do for him."

"You want me to find him," I said. It was not really a question.

"Yes."

"I don't know anything about Mexico or illegal aliens or coyotes, Leah."

"I've thought about this a lot, Carl. We can't turn to the authorities. Stella is an illegal too. If I tried to ask anyone official for help, Stella would be deported. That's no big deal with Mexicans, you know. If they want to deport a

German, say, they have to go through all sorts of court hearings and formal charges and I don't know what all else. But if it's just a Mexican, they just round them up and put them on a bus or a plane and ship them south. If that happened to Stella, it would just make things worse for the whole family. She provides most of the income for them, little as it is.

"I told you to begin with, Carl, that I wasn't here making a play on your sympathies. Lord knows you don't owe me anything," she looked me square in the eyes, "or vice versa. I intend to pay you."

I tried to say something, but she wouldn't let me interrupt. This was something she had all worked out, and she was going to have her say about it.

"I haven't much cash anymore, Carl. The medical coverage Mac pays for doesn't cover quite everything. The way it's set up, my estate will sell the house and use that income to pay off the medical bills. There should be enough to cover it unless something really unusual comes up at . . . the last minute. Anything left over is willed to Stella.

"I also have a twenty-five-thousand-dollar term life policy that is paid up to age fifty." She smiled. "They can't cancel it, and I don't really have to worry about it expiring before I need it."

Jesus, that must be a hard thing to accept. Leah seemed to be doing it just fine.

"Mac was the original beneficiary of the policy, but as the policy owner I have the right to name anyone or anything I damn well please. For obvious reasons, that won't be L. Ron MacPherson."

No surprise there. The son of a bitch.

"I've already contacted the insurance company. I've split

the payout sixty–forty between Stella and you, Carl. Fifteen thousand dollars to her after my death and ten thousand to you. I would have offered it to you in cash except that I just don't have it."

Christ, she was just as serious as she could be. Sitting here talking about getting me some damned money just as soon as she corked off. Which wouldn't be but a few months from now.

I looked at her and realized that there were a whole lot of things I could have said, countless ways I could respond.

None of them seemed to cover what I was thinking and what I was feeling.

I just didn't know what I could tell her.

I also just didn't know any way I could turn her down.

Not the money part of it. That I could take or get along very nicely without, however it seemed to work out the best for Leah's pride. I really didn't care about that.

What was tearing me up, though, was that this was a woman I still thought of as awfully special.

What I really *wanted* to do was to take her in my arms and comfort her and assure her that everything would be all right.

But that would be a lie.

Everything *wasn't* going to be all right. Leah was going to die a very rough death, and the person she loved most in all the world was hurting, and that knowledge was hurting Leah.

There probably wasn't a chance in ten thousand that I could do anything to ease *any* of her several pains. There was no chance that I could do anything to ease the physical part of it. There was only the faintest likelihood that I could ease any of the emotional hurting.

I looked at this disease-racked shell of the woman I had

once loved, and I just couldn't convince myself that all of that feeling was dead.

"I'll try," I told her. "I can't make you any promises. But I'll try."

I was very grateful to her for one thing. She accepted that solemnly and seriously, the way I had meant it, with no surge of sudden and possibly very false hope.

But then, Leah Crowder already knew more than most people about false hopes and groundless joys.

"Thank you, Carl."

4

We had lunch and I followed Leah on the several-hour trip out along the river to Cotopaxi. She was driving a middle-aged Coupe de Ville these days, which seemed unlike her. Back when I had known her well, which was before small cars became the seminecessity they are now, she had always chosen small, spritely, jazzy little automobiles by preference. I was wondering about this small change in her, whether it might have been caused by the years with stuffy Mac, when a thought came to me. I asked her, the next time she stopped, which was fairly often. Every half-hour or so she would find a place to pull over so she could get out of the heavy, oversprung car and walk around for a few moments.

She looked embarrassed when she answered. "I had an absolutely adorable TR-7 that stayed with me in the settlement, but I just can't take much bouncing and bumping anymore. Gertrude here," she pointed toward the Caddie, "rides like a cloud and has power *every*thing. Besides, nobody wants old boats like this now. I came out about four thousand dollars to the good when I got rid of my Triumph and bought Gertrude."

I looked at Leah then with maybe a little more awareness and a little more respect. The kind of pain she had now, the constancy of it, was something that I could not really begin to understand. She was still quite a girl, I thought.

We turned off U.S. 50 and crossed the bridge at Cotopaxi, and I followed the pale lemon Coupe de Ville out past the school to Leah's house, formerly also the home of L. Ron MacPherson. It was a low, modern, brick affair set inside a fence that would contain maybe eight or ten acres of scrub grass, yucca, and small cacti. I didn't see any hobby-sized barn or shed or pens around, so it wasn't a yen for livestock or the country-squire thing that had brought them to the country. The garage door raised itself as we drove in, presumably by way of one of those remote-control gadgets, and I parked in the graveled circle drive while Leah drove on into the garage. That, too, I realized, would be a potential eliminator of minor pains.

"You can come in this way, Carl."

I trailed obediently through the garage. It was a two-car shelter, but now only one seemed to be in use. There was a workbench on the back wall with rows of empty pegs and nails close to hand. There were some oddly patterned clean spots on the work surface and some empty bolt holes showing where Mac's toys had once been. A hose and some long-handled garden tools were on the side wall, but there didn't seem to be much in the way of mower, snow blower, or the like. I wondered if Leah was aware of the oddity of the garage's nearly sterile neatness and decided she probably was not.

Stella was in the kitchen. The kitchen was neat enough and modern enough that it could have been brought to life off the pages of *House Beautiful* or some similar publication. Stella, though, was not exactly the way I had pictured her in my mind.

Somehow I had decided that she would be plump and jolly and a bit matronly at the same time. Uniformed almost certainly, although I had not yet pictured whether the uniform was to be that of a maid or a nurse.

Instead she was a dark-haired girl of probably twenty in jeans, sneakers, and a yellow T-shirt with the silk-screened message: "Be patient, God isn't through with me yet." She was very thin, to be honest, rather homely, with an undershot jaw and slightly protruding upper teeth. But there was genuine warmth and concern and pleasure in her eyes when Leah got home.

Stella gave Leah a careful, gentle hug of welcome and guided the older woman—only very slightly older, I kept having to remind myself—to a seat at the kitchen table. Within seconds she was preparing a cup of tea with cream for Leah and was inquiring what I might like.

The kind of concern she was showing for Leah was not the sort of thing you can hire anyone to do for you. It was for reals, as a child of my acquaintance used to put it, and I discovered that I liked Stella already.

The next time I looked at her, as she was bringing me a cup of black coffee, I discovered that I was no longer seeing her as a homely girl. Just as a very nice one.

That is something that is a habit of mine anyway. The first time I meet someone I see what they look like on the outside. But after that I tend to see them as I perceive them to be on the inside. I once knew a woman who was, to be blunt about it, fat. She was fat and had mannish features and small eyes set too close together, and when I first met her I thought she was one of the most physically unattractive females I had ever met. That was the only time I ever saw her like that. For the next several years, until she moved away and we lost contact, I knew she was one of the loveliest, nicest people I had ever been privileged to know.

It was like that now with Stella Cervantes, and I was pleased that she had been here to help a very special lady through the rough times.

"This is Mr. Heller, Stella. Carl is the friend I've been telling you about."

"Will you help us, Mr. Heller?" A stereotype bit the dust, so to speak. Her English was as good as mine and almost totally devoid of accent. I would have been willing to bet that Stella watched a lot of television, that great destroyer of the regional accent in modern America.

"I'll try, Stella. I told Leah, and I have to tell you the same thing. I can't make any promises or offer any guarantees. I can only try."

Again there was a calm acceptance of the fact without any display of false hope. I liked that about Stella. I also wondered whether she had learned it from Leah or if it might have been the other way around. If it was something this young girl had been able to give to Leah, it was a gift I would like to help repay to her and her family.

"Would you sit with us, please, Stella? I want you to tell me everything you know about your brother's—Julio, is it?—plans to cross the border."

She fixed a cup of tea for herself and joined us, and the three of us talked until dusk was turning into full night.

It was conversation about things that were totally alien to me. Much more so than a few lousy miles would seem able to make possible.

The coyote had been paid five hundred dollars. Five hundred U.S. dollars. Just to take somebody across a river and put them on a bus on the other side.

Incredible.

To me it was something that should be worth just about the two-cent toll it costs to walk across the international bridge linking El Paso and Juárez. To Julio it had been a dangerous and costly venture that might well have cost him his life.

"It is safer," Stella said when I couldn't help asking why. "The *chotas* are everywhere near the border. *La migra*. The Border Patrol. They are very smart. Sometimes the coyotes are smarter. That is what they are paid for."

"It isn't easy," Leah said. Then she turned to Stella and asked, "Do you mind if I tell him about your experience?" The girl seemed to withdraw into herself, but she nodded her approval.

"When Stella came over, Carl, she didn't have the money for a coyote. She came across the Black Bridge. You don't know about that? It's quite famous in its own way. It's the railroad bridge between Juárez and El Paso. The Border Patrol waits on one side and the would-be illegals on the other. When the patrolmen get tired of the game or are called away to go somewhere else, the people run across the bridge. They know they will probably be picked up on this side and sent back anyway, but they make the run, and if they are lucky they might get far enough into the country to avoid *la migra*.

"When Stella came over she didn't have any money with her. She ran across the bridge and walked to New Mexico.

Somewhere out by the race track, apparently. Sunland, I think it is."

I nodded. I'd heard of Sunland Park. They run Quarter Horses there every season, and I read about them in the *Quarter Horse Journal*.

"A motorist picked her up and offered her a ride, Carl. He said he was going to Albuquerque. A few miles up the road there were some Border Patrol men. The man told Stella he would be able to hide her and take her on with him if she agreed to be 'nice' to him. I don't know if you would call it rape or not. He didn't actually use force on the poor child. Whatever you want to call it, he used her three times between Sunland Park and Albuquerque, then he dumped her out and went on his merry way. That was a couple months before Mac found her and hired her. The time in between wasn't particularly pleasant for her either."

"Even so, Mr. Heller, I am one of the very lucky ones. I am here in this wonderful place with Leah, and I am alive. Very many, possibly Julio too, are not able to cross alive."

"Look," I said, "I'm having a little trouble trying to understand this. I've seen the Rio Grande down that way. There sure isn't any danger of drowning. What can be so dangerous about crossing? I mean, if you do get caught over here you're just sent back. Nobody is going to shoot you, for crying out loud."

"*La migra* will not shoot, no, Mr. Heller, but there are others who would."

"Who would it be that important to, Stella? That's what I don't understand."

She shrugged. "There are bandits, for one thing. Illegals are safe prey for them. There is no one a wetback can complain to, you know, and most who cross take with them everything they can in the hope they will be able to buy their way far from the border and live until they can find work.

"The coyotes themselves will shoot the illegals or let them die if they fear they might be caught. The business is very large, the money very important to them. More important than the lives of a few more wets."

"Five hundred dollars? It isn't that much, Stella."

"Five hundred? Possibly not, Mr. Heller. But we are not speaking now of five hundred dollars. We are speaking of a great many payments of five hundred dollars. You thought the coyote brought over only one illegal at a time?"

"Yeah, I guess I did."

"No, Mr. Heller. He will bring over a dozen at a time. Twenty. Sometimes more. Ten thousand dollars for the night's work, Mr. Heller. There are many men who would kill to protect that amount. Kill to keep from being arrested and put out of the business."

I whistled. Ten thousand or more, damn.

"They bundle the illegals into the backs of trucks, into milk tanks, into all manner of hiding places. If the coyote thinks he is to be caught, he will abandon the carrier and run away. The wetbacks may be discovered and released by *la migra*. They may stay there instead to suffocate or die of poison fumes. It makes no difference to the coyote. He has already gotten his fee. And he has run away to collect more fees the following day.

"*La migra* has very powerful listening things along the border, Mr. Heller. Very modern equipment. If the coyote thinks some frightened illegal is going to give him away, why not eliminate the problem the easiest way possible." She sighed. "People die on your border every week of the year, Mr. Heller. The crossing is *very* dangerous."

"Why in the world would they risk it then, Stella?"

"They are hungry, Mr. Heller."

Jesus. How do you respond to that.

It seemed incredible to me, sitting there surrounded by all manner of affluence, every bit as well fed as I chose to be at any moment of every day.

We fuss and complain about the damned illegals coming over here taking jobs away from our citizens when there is so much unemployment.

There is probably a very sound argument there. In the abstract. But Stella wasn't an abstraction for me. She was a very nice, very warm, very good human being who was sitting in a chair at the same table with me.

Somehow I just didn't feel like I could look at her and be angry with her because somewhere down by the river there was an unemployed Mary Doe who could have used this same work.

Mary Doe, I kept remembering now, was drawing food stamps and unemployment compensation and aid to dependent children and maybe half a dozen other things to help her along until she could find work.

Stella and Julio and the thousands of other people like them didn't have that to lean on.

"They are hungry," Stella had said.

Somehow, civic duty or no, I just couldn't make myself despise a man for trying to put food in his kids' bellies.

And somehow I found myself preferring the term *wetback*—racist as it might sound—to *illegal*.

For damn sure these people hadn't done anything that deserved a death penalty.

I looked at the two women across the table from me. "I think," I said, "I would like to have a talk with some coyotes."

5

We had a bit of an argument about who was going to do what. Since my command of Spanish is pretty much limited to *taco*, *burrito*, and *enchilada*, I would have welcomed Stella's company on the trip, but she was just plain scared to be that close to the border without a green card in her possession.

I could accept that easily enough. What I didn't want to do was take Leah along with me.

"Those are dangerous people, Leah. You don't know what might happen."

That was a damn-fool thing to say, as I realized just about the time I said it.

"Carl, you thought it would be safe enough for Stella. Besides," she added with a chuckle, "I have less to lose than anyone else. A month? Big deal. I'm going."

"I don't like it, Leah."

"I've heard they have a new laetrile-based drug available down there, Carl. Who knows, this whole experience could be very good for me."

"Dammit, Leah, you know I don't have an argument to counter that."

"Of course I know it, silly. Why do you think I used it?"

I hadn't the faintest idea if she was woofing me about that or not. I certainly would not have put it past her.

"If you go along, Leah, we'd have to take that damned Cadillac, and a Jeep could come in awfully handy down there if I have to get off the roads somewhere."

"Now you're making excuses," she said. "If you think you might need the Jeep, by all means we will take the Jeep. Believe me, I've already put up with more discomfort than that."

I sighed. "We'll take your car."

"We?"

"We," I agreed. "Do you need any, uh, special attention . . . ?"

"What? Oh. Not really. I don't need a colostomy bag or anything like that. I'll be fine, Carl. Truly. Why, I can dress myself and everything."

"I didn't mean it like that, darn it."

She looked skeptical. But then maybe she had good reason to. After all, I had no idea what she had had to put up with from people already.

"Look, I don't think we ought to wait around any longer than necessary. If that's all right with you. I need to go home and pack. Make arrangements for my neighbor to watch the ranch. Like that. I could pick you up tomorrow morning about, oh, eight o'clock. Okay?"

"You're sure you can get away? I know you have animals to take care of and everything. I don't want this to be a problem for you."

The girl sure was a worrier. "It's fine," I assured her. "The horses have plenty of graze, and Walter—you remember him, probably—he'll make sure there's water in the stock tank for them. The cattle I just leave out to earn their own living the year round." I smiled at her. "You never met my granddad, but he always used to tell me the problems with the beef industry started when men let their cattle depend on a man for their living instead of the man depending on the cows for his. That's why I like the Longhorn breed. They still know how to do for themselves."

"You're really doing it then, Carl, just the way you always wanted to."

"Uh-huh. All of it."

"I'm glad for you." Again there was a moment when I thought she was going to reach out to touch me, but she remained motionless, her hands cupped around the teacup Stella had brought her.

The moment passed before I was sure it had really been, and she turned to Stella. "I want you to call your cousin in Juárez tonight. Ask her to help us if Carl needs her. And I'll get her address and number. Remind me to write that down."

Stella nodded. She had been quiet since refusing to go along to El Paso. I expect she was embarrassed and probably thought she was letting Leah down.

"Actually," I told the girl, "that probably will work out a lot better than if you were with us. A local would know what's going on a lot better than you could. And I assume your kinfolk speak Spanish."

Stella looked startled for a moment. Finally she realized that I was trying to make a joke. Her expression softened somewhat.

It felt strange—and actually kinda nice for a change—to be driving a big, heavy road machine like that old Coupe de Ville. Leah had been right about the car. It rode like a cloud in the jetstream.

It slid down I-25 with an effortless grace, and once we waved goodbye to the last of the Colorado bears going up Raton Pass and crossed into New Mexico, I used the cruise-control button to ease the speed up to seventy-five or thereabouts.

That is one of the good things you can say about New Mexico. They have an enlightened attitude about the double-nickle down there. If you ain't actually aiming at pedestrians with malicious intent, the New Mexico cops tend to leave you alone regardless of your indicated groundspeed. The poe-lice in my beloved Colorado, on the other hand, will nail you for sixty or more, and the stretch of interstate between Walsenburg and Trinidad is a particularly good hunting ground for them. I long ago learned to take it easy down that way.

We stopped for a quick, early lunch at the Burger King near the second Raton exit. I wasn't really all that hungry yet myself, but it's a long haul between Raton and the next waterhole south.

I settled Leah in a booth and went to fetch us some Whoppers and cold drinks. "You're awfully quiet this morning," I said when I got back with the laden tray.

"I'm all right." She picked up her burger and disrobed it, getting rid of the lettuce and tomato and pickles. It occurred to me that my casual eating habits might not sit so well with her physical condition.

"I'm all right, I told you," she snapped when I asked her.

"Yes, ma'am."

I was about halfway through the Whopper—not quite as greasy-good as the ones you can get at the Lake George Inn back home but just fine all the same—when I happened to remember something.

Good old Carl. Every bit as thoughtful and considerate as your average sadist.

Yesterday, driving home, Leah had had to stop every little while to move around and try to ease her pains. And here I'd been rolling down the highway on cruise control, not a care in the flippin' world. Damn! The woman was hurting, and I was blithely doing my thing. Talk about your basic idiot . . . !

After that we stopped every little while. At the public rest area near Maxwell, at Wagon Mound, Las Vegas—they have one of those in New Mexico, too—beside the Pecos. It made for a very relaxed trip, I found. It also seemed to help Leah. Thank goodness. It also made the going rather slower than I was used to.

Normally I consider the run from home to El Paso a single day's ride, on two wheels or four. This time the fatigue that was graying Leah's face made me pull it in far short of the border. By the time we reached Albuquerque I was looking for a motel. We settled on a generic, nonchain operation that advertised low rates on their neon sign. Leah's choice. I pulled up under the concrete-and-steel canopy outside the office and started to get out of the car.

"Wait."

"Yeah?"

"Here." She dipped into her purse and came out with a wad of cash.

"The expenses are mine; the fee is yours," I said. "That's one of the rules."

"Please, Carl. I insist."

I shook my head and ducked away from the car before she could say anything else.

The motel wasn't close to full at the early evening hour, and I had no trouble getting us connecting rooms.

Later, after a supper during which Leah ate very little, I picked up a six-pack of Coors from a convenience market down the block and carried a pair of cold ones into her room. She used to like the stuff, I remembered.

"Join me?"

"All right." She had kicked off her shoes and was stretched out on the hard rental bed with both skimpy pillows propped behind her head. I handed her a can and took a seat on the lone chair that was provided for the customers. Leah took a swallow of beer and closed her eyes. She looked awfully tired.

Looking at her lying there, in the connotation of motel room and anonymous bed, brought back memories I thought had been buried long, long ago.

She had been so vital then, so vibrant. So eager. Often playful.

She liked to tussle and tickle and laugh. And without warning the laughter would end. Her breath would catch in her throat. Her eyes—just as lovely now as they had been then—would soften and the lids would droop heavily with the weight of a greedy passion for the pleasures of her flesh. She had *always* been, I remembered uncomfortably now, moistly lubricious when her eyes did that.

She was still attractive. Different on the outside. Just as lovely inside, where it counted.

I looked at her and felt myself growing hard in spite of my best and mostly gentlemanly intentions.

Dammit, Leah probably needed the nuisance of a horny suitor just about as much as she needed a fresh form of cancer.

She had already told me that the chemotherapy had wiped out her sex drive. If that hint hadn't been plain enough for me, well, maybe the next time she ought to use a ball peen hammer. Applied between the eyes.

"Carl?" She sounded startled.

I'd been so wrapped up in my thinking and remembering that I hadn't realized she had opened her eyes again and was staring at me.

More specifically, she was staring at the slight but unmistakable bulge in my slacks. Why, I asked myself, hadn't I worn jeans to travel, the way I usually did.

"Are you really . . . ?"

I thought about standing up to get away, but that just would have been worse. Instead, I slouched down into the damned chair and crossed my legs. I could feel my ears getting warm. "I'm sorry, Leah. I didn't mean to . . . offend you." My lousy ears were definitely turning traitor now. The heat was spreading all over my face.

Leah sat up and laughed.

Jesus! I felt like I must be glowing like Rudolph's nose.

"Oh, Carl."

"Yeah?" I mumbled. I wasn't looking at her.

"Thank you."

"What?"

"You couldn't possibly be faking that blush. I know you too well for that." She laughed again. "We do know each other rather well still, don't we?"

"Yeah."

"Thank you."

At least this odd line of conversation was removing my problem. It would be possible to make a semidignified escape pretty soon. "I don't understand," I told her.

"Carl, you are an absolute dear."

"Hell, woman, everybody knows that. But I still don't understand what this 'thank you' jazz is supposed to be."

Leah laughed again. This time I didn't find it so bloody embarrassing.

"You were looking at me just then like I was an actual women, Carl. Don't you understand that?"

"Oh, I was real well aware of that, lady. In fact, it might be a lot easier in the future if we don't get connecting rooms. I . . . still think a bunch of you, you know."

Damned if she didn't start to look a little bit weepy. She took a hasty swallow of her beer, and a couple tears escaped and began to roll down her cheeks. She wiped them off impatiently but with no phony attempt at hiding them. "That reaction of yours, dear Carl, was the very nicest compliment I've had in, well, I can't remember how long."

I was still puzzled. Maybe it showed.

"I have cancer, Carl." She sounded like that was supposed to explain everything.

"I believe you mentioned that before, Leah."

"You really don't understand, do you?" She smiled. "Then thank you for that, too." Leah sighed and set the can aside. She swung her legs—still quite good legs, and the way her skirt had hiked up, there was no way I could help noticing that fact—off the bed so she could sit facing me.

"That was the first time in a very long while, Carl, that anyone has looked at me like I was a genuine member of the human race. In that way, anyhow."

"My gosh, Leah, you're a good-looking woman."

"Carl, when you have cancer you aren't regarded as a desirable anything. And I don't mean just in bed. I don't mean anything having to do with the gross place where my breast used to be. It never gets that far anyway, dear. I mean just in polite company.

"When you have cancer, people tend to think of you as being contagious. Having cancer nowadays is the same social thrill that being a leper used to be."

"Come on, Leah. I can't hardly believe that."

The abrupt little bark of laughter this time was definitely bitter. "One of the really good clues, my dear ignorant former love, is when you go to a party with your husband and the hostess serves everyone in lovely crystal glassware. Except for you. Your beverage comes in a paper cup." The pull at her lips that probably was intended to be a smile had not a hint of mirth in it.

"Did that really . . . ?" I stopped and shook my head.

"Oh, yes, dear. And a lot more just like it."

I took the few paces across the room to sit beside her and wrap my arms around her. I held her and rocked her and could feel the heat of her tears through the thin material of my shirt. Her slim shoulders shuddered under my touch.

It was, I realized suddenly, the first time I had physically touched her since we had met. She hadn't offered to shake hands even. She had been holding herself slightly apart the entire time. I hadn't even noticed it until now.

She had gotten so used to rejection that she had assumed it. I was sure of that.

I shifted position and pulled her gently down beside me on the bed. Her eyes were closed and she was still crying.

"Leah." She continued to sob.

"Look at me, Leah."

Her eyes opened. Dark gold in a pain-racked face.

I bent and kissed her, deeply and lingeringly. The taste of her was as sweet as I had remembered it to be. "Did you know, ma'am, that I never quit loving you?"

She pulled away and began to cry harder than ever. I didn't know what to do. I didn't want to hurt her in any way. I would have gotten up, thinking the contact might be bothering her, but she was clinging to me with a fierce strength.

After a moment she turned back and offered her mouth.

This time when I kissed her it was like all those intervening years had never happened.

I stroked her head and throat and looked into those lovely, luminous, golden brown eyes.

There was no way I could hide that same insistent reaction. She had to be able to feel the damn thing bumping against her stomach.

I sat up and reached rather shakily for a cigarette. I thought Leah was crying again, but I didn't look to see. "I think," I said, "that it is one of the world's greater wastes, this side effect you were telling me about where the sex drive is lost."

Leah laughed. It was a nice-sounding laugh this time. "Dear Carl, I did tell you that, didn't I? Did I not mention that it is a *temporary* effect? They gave up on my chemo months ago, dear."

"You're kidding."

"Why would I lie to you, dear." Leah was smirking. She seemed quite pleased with herself.

But only for a moment. A cloud of unhappiness veiled her eyes, and she withdrew from me slightly.

"What is it?"

She shook her head impatiently. Then she brightened. I could see quite plainly that she was forcing it. She slipped off the bed and knelt by my feet, reaching for my zipper.

"What . . . ?" I stopped her.

"Please, Carl. You don't want to see me undressed. You really don't. But I can fix you up, dear." She wasn't looking at me and was still trying to get to my zipper. "I'm sure it's just like riding a bicycle, dear. And I promise not to bite."

"Dammit, what makes you think I've gotten that selfish in my old age?"

"Really . . ."

"You're right. *Really!* Get your clothes off. You want to go down on me then? Fine. I'll help you. But I get to play all the same games that you do, lady. We aren't starting any solitary sports here. Huh-uh. No way."

She looked like she didn't much believe it, but she didn't fight me when I peeled her clothes off.

Later, quite a bit later, I had time to pet and hold her while we rested.

I ran a fingertip over the scars where her right breast had been. It was mildly disconcerting at first, but no more than that. The only really distressing thing, quickly accepted, was the absence of a nipple. That and all the fleshy tissue had had to be removed. The skin showed mottled red where the grafts had been placed, and there was a more-or-less L-shaped scar corresponding to where the bottom and right side of the breast had been.

"Gross, huh? Bull. It all depends on your point of view. If this hadn't been done, lovely person, you probably wouldn't be here romping on a wide, wide bed with me right now." I smiled at her. "Viva la modified radicals, lady." I bent and kissed her scars.

Leah started to cry again.

This time, odd as it might seem, it had kind of a nice sound about it. I stroked her and held her close and was glad to be with her.

6

We checked into the Paso del Norte—one room, thank you—just a few blocks from the international bridge. I prefer to avoid taking vehicles across into a border town. It can be such a hassle getting them back home.

The del Norte is one of those very old hotels that has been modernized to keep up with the times, but modern furniture and plumbing can't hide the immensely tall ceilings that tell the story of its age. The bellman showed us where to click this and turn that, deposited our bags on the two double beds in the huge room, accepted his tip, and left. I gathered Leah in for some smooching in the privacy newly offered. She didn't seem to mind.

"Got time for a quickie, lady?"

She seemed to have lost her shyness about her body very nicely. Her answer was immediate and very direct.

When we were back to a reasonably normal rate of respiration, Leah assigned herself the left bank of drawers in the broad dresser and gave me the right side.

"What are you, some kind of neatnik? There isn't anything wrong with living out of a suitcase, you know."

"Slob," she accused with a smile. "Go ahead and make like a chimney. I'll unpack for both of us."

If she expected gentlemanly protest she was in for a

disappointment. I grinned at her and reached for a cigarette. The bottom of the ashtray was cold on my belly but convenient there. I enjoyed watching her while she opened the bags and busied around from bed to dresser to bathroom and back.

"Carl?" She sounded uneasy.

"Um?"

"I didn't think . . . Do you really believe you might need this?" She had a delicate, two-fingered grip on the butt of my Smith & Wesson M59. She was holding it the way she might have picked up a wad of soiled toilet paper. I had forgotten about having it in my suitcase, actually.

"I always travel with it. Nearly always, anyhow."

"It isn't loaded, is it?"

"Of course it's loaded."

She made a face.

"Do that again."

"What?"

"That face. I swear, you're cute as a new calf."

She stuck her tongue out at me.

"Wrong face," I told her. She did it again.

"What do you want me to do with this thing?"

I shrugged, set aside the ashtray, and went to take the pistol from her. I checked to make sure she hadn't accidentally taken the safety off, then tucked the bluntly efficient Smith into my top dresser drawer under some jockey shorts Leah had neatly folded and put in there.

Leah was looking serious again. "Do you really think you might need that, Carl?"

"I have no idea, honey. Everyone is afraid these people might have killed Stella's brother. I'd just as soon they didn't do the same for me." I realized, too late, how that might sound to a person who was dying of cancer, but Leah came to my rescue.

She held me close and applied a fluttering of butterfly kisses to my neck and chest. "In that case," she said, "I'm glad you brought the gun, dear. I don't want it to happen to you either."

I went back to my smoke, and she went back to her efforts to organize the hotel room into a degree of comfort much greater than I usually bothered with in strange surroundings.

"Hungry?" she asked when she was done.

"Approximately starved."

She grinned.

"What was that about?"

"Just remembering. Good loving always did give you an appetite."

"You pick strange things to remember, lady."

"I also remember that the pattern used to be to make love, then have something to eat, then go back to making love, lover."

I smiled at her. "Shall we see if that pattern's been changed?"

It hadn't changed at all, I was pleased to discover.

7

The main drag of Juárez—at least I assume it's the main drag; it's all I'd ever seen of the place the few times I had been there before—is, to be blunt about it, gaudy. And busy. Lordy, but it is both gaudy and busy.

Bright colors, bright sunshine, a constantly flowing sea of humanity . . . it is well nigh incredible. Block after block of tiny shops grab for your attention, trying to sell you sandals and saddles, T-shirts and teapots, whiskey and jewelry and toys and knives and hats and even, so help me, furniture made out of steer horns and upholstered in velvet. I almost bought a chair made in that abnormal fashion. The damn thing was so ugly it was nearly irresistible. Leah provided an anchor to reality and dragged me away before I could make a fool of myself. More of one than usual, that is.

The street is absolutely solid with slowly moving vehicles and slowly milling people. Vendors peddling cigarettes—U.S. brands at well under half the U.S. prices; try to figure that one because I sure can't—and perfectly illegal-in-the-U.S. switchblade knives and snowcones and candy and probably anything else that could be considered more or less portable.

Tourists are everywhere, taking advantage of the peso's

wildly inflation-battered rates, haggling with shopkeepers and forking over gaudy wads of U.S. currency for equally gaudy doodads and bric-a-brac.

Mexicans, locals and would-be wetbacks, too, are everywhere, selling, buying, moving steadily up and down the noisy, busy blocks of the border district. Not too many of them here *looked* all that hungry. They were dressed just like anybody on the other side of the border.

It was an utter madhouse of a place.

Oddly enough, as much as I detest cities and crowds usually, there is something about a border town that is infectious in its air of busy excitement. I *like* Juárez, and I can't figure out why.

Leah and I walked into the middle of it all and stood on a street corner for a time breathing in the atmosphere of the place. I had offered to drive her over, but she said lately she was finding walking to be actually more comfortable for her than riding in a car. I don't think she had ever had reason to learn about my aversion to driving across the border, so I accepted that and we walked.

The bars were all open and apparently busy in spite of the early morning hour. We had spent a night in exhausted sleep, had a marvelous breakfast at the del Norte, and were finally getting around to the reason we had come here.

Leah had tried to call Stella's cousin, or whatever, from the hotel, but I had nipped that in time to prevent it. "I've had some bad experiences trusting telephones too much," I told her. "It would be better to call her from a pay phone on the other side. And not tell her anything then but where and when to meet us." She gave me an odd look but did as I asked.

"So, smart alec, where's a telephone?" she asked me now.

"In there." I hooked a thumb toward the nearest bar. I had never been inside the place, but hell, bars always have telephones, don't they? This one did, on a side wall. The place was dark and gave an impression of coolness that may have been accurate or may as easily have been a false signal caused by the shadowy interior. One thing Juárez generally is is hot. The bar smelled of beer and liquor and aftershave. No hookers, I noticed, despite the reputation of all border-town joints. Just a bunch of apparently serious drinkers going at it.

Leah made her call from the pay phone while I slouched against the wall wondering if I had been right to put up so little protest when she had wanted to come along. Some of the patrons of this place looked like they could be bad news if they took a notion to.

Still, Juárez and all the cities like it make their way in this world by tolling in the tourist dollars. Trouble for the greenback-laden Yanks is frowned upon. We probably were safer here than on the walk from the bridge back to the Paso del Norte.

The call took only moments. Leah did not look especially pleased when she hung up.

"Well?"

"I could use a cup of coffee."

"Now that," I said, "is a full and complete report."

"In a minute," she said. "I'm, uh, not entirely comfortable here." She glanced nervously toward the bar, where a couple hard-looking types were making no attempt to hide the once-over they were giving her.

If Leah hadn't been there I might have done something to remind them of their manners. But then if Leah hadn't been there, there would not have been any need of it. I told myself to remember my own manners and got her out of there.

"So speak," I said when we were back on the sidewalk.

"Stella's cousin wasn't home," she said. "I talked to her eldest. Thank God, he speaks English. I tried to get Stella to teach me some Spanish, but it just didn't work. My fault, not hers."

"Would you mind terribly if I asked you to get to the point?"

"Oh, that," she said with mock boredom. "He will call the cousin. Her name is Carmen, by the way. She'll meet us for lunch. I asked him to pick a very quiet place. He said she will meet us at La Florida. It's supposed to be on the strip here somewhere."

"I saw it. A couple blocks back, I think. What time?"

"He was kind of vague about that. Twelve-ten. He said that would give her time to get there on her lunch break."

We spent the intervening time shopping. Leah hadn't let me buy the chair of my dreams, so I wouldn't let her buy me a hand-tooled saddle with one of those dinner-plate-sized saddlehorns that they favor—or used to favor—down that way.

We compromised by her buying me a really elegant suede poncho decorated with spur and horsehead designs and by her allowing me to gift her with a genuinely lovely gold filigree necklace. Solid 24K, the man said very early in the negotiations.

That one kind of wiped Leah out, and for a while there we had some tears to contend with. She kept trying to tell me that a gold wash would do just as well since she wouldn't have enough time for it to turn her neck green, and I kept telling her to shut up, that I could buy my favorite lady a bauble if I damn well wanted to. The shopkeeper looked like he was not following all this, which was understandable, but he was on my side, and between us we were able to win her over. Once the purchase was made, she allowed as how she loved the thing and expected to never take it off, X rays excepted of course. That crack had me thinking about crying too, but I didn't.

Slightly before noon we found the restaurant and joined the very thin trickle of folks going there for lunch. Not at all the number of people you would expect to choose a given place when there were so many people who would be looking for a lunch spot, and I couldn't help but wonder if this was some kind of ptomaine specialty house we had been pointed toward.

Then we stepped inside, and I discovered that I'd been just about 180 degrees off course when I had thought that.

Son of a gun. From the outside it was just your same old storefront with peeling paint, some curtains at the windows, and a sign saying you could find chow there.

Inside it was like we had stepped from the flagrantly honky-tonk atmosphere of Juárez to a fine Parisian restaurant. My idea of what a restaurant in Paris ought to look like anyhow; I've never actually seen one.

Impeccable nappery. Impeccably groomed and dressed waiters who were dressed as well in an aura of polite dignity. A total atmosphere of, well, elegance.

Blew me away, it did. I think Leah was just as surprised.

The maître d'—I wouldn't think of calling him a head waiter—showed us to a table for four in a cozy corner away from the street, and someone else—darned if I'd know what to call him—delivered menus with offerings like quail on toast and lobster tail. The prices—Leah's menu didn't have any prices listed—were modest, though probably pretty tall by local standards.

Leah started to giggle.

"Hush, woman, you're fixing to embarrass me."

She didn't quit.

"All right, what is it?"

"Care for some Mexican food, Carl?"

I didn't get it for a moment. Then I searched the menu again. There wasn't a single item of Mexican food to be found.

"Hush and resign yourself to eating civilized, woman."

"But I *like* Mexican food."

I grinned at her. "So do I, but don't worry. We can always eat Mexican back across the border."

A young, very handsome fellow filled our water glasses, and another man brought a tray of relishes. So far we hadn't been visited by the same fellow twice.

There was a break in that pattern when the maître d' presented himself at our table with a slight bow. He excused himself to me for the interruption, then asked Leah if she might be Ms. Crowder. His English, right down to the "miz", was perfect.

"I have a message, Miz Crowder. Your party will not be able to join you at luncheon. Would you please call again this evening to make arrangements." He bowed himself away from the table.

Leah looked disappointed. "I suppose we could go, since Carmen won't be meeting us here."

"And miss an opportunity like this? No chance, ma'am."

We dined and we wined, and the food was as excellent as the service, and that left absolutely nothing to be desired. It was all for darn sure like the rich folks must have it, and I was glad to be sharing it with Leah.

Afterward she said she was getting tired. Which worked out well, really. I wanted to take a closer, more critical look at Juárez without all the touristy distractions competing for my attention. I bundled the lady into a cab—it is no problem at all popping back and forth across the border in a taxi, unlike the problems you can have when you drive yourself north across it—and kissed her goodbye.

"Promise me you'll be careful," she said just before the cab pulled away.

"Aw, I'm all grown up now, Leah. What possible trouble could I get into?"

Gee, that can be a stupid question.

8

I walked back north toward the border. In the crush of traffic the cab couldn't move any faster than I was going afoot, and for several blocks I could see Leah sitting in the back of the cab, talking with the driver, unaware that I was still so near. I liked having an opportunity to admire her without her knowing I was looking at her. It occurred to me that I was enjoying looking at *this* Leah now, with no substitutions of past, remembered images getting in the way. She had changed a good deal, in ways that were beyond the physical changes, and I liked the lady possibly more now than I had before.

The cab veered to the right to join the line of vehicles slowly trickling into and through the customs shed, and I crossed the street in mid-block to walk west along the thin trickle of water that was the famous Rio Grande.

The Rio must be a darn well-used stream, because the few times I've seen it down this far it has held mighty little water. I'm told that it does carry a heavy flow some times of the year, and then they have problems with drownings when the wets try to cross over to the U.S. side. But every time I've seen it, which has not been very many, it has been low enough to walk across.

Up farther, of course, up around Los Alamos, where I've also seen it, it runs bank-full and fast. Not quite wild enough for really exciting rafting, but a real handful for anyone who might want to swim across.

I walked a block or so west of the bridge and stopped to loiter and look.

The Black Bridge was there, dark and rusty-looking although I could see how it would have gotten its nickname.

On the Juárez end a group of Mexican idlers sat, smoking and talking and relaxing in the sunshine. Some of them were carrying bags of candy or fruit that they dipped into from time to time for a munch. Most of them were men, young men mostly, but there were a few women in the group too. None of them looked to be all that tense, although of course you can't always tell from looking. We all try on masks to hide our fears from the world.

Yet these people were Mexican citizens who were doing their level best to become illegal aliens in the United States. They were determined to break our laws and participate in our bounty. I found myself wishing them well.

Over on the far side, parked in plain sight, I could see a light green Chevy Blazer with a light bar on top and some sort of decal or emblem on the door. It was too far away for me to see what the waiting Border Patrol men were doing in their four-wheel-drive cruiser, but I imagined they might also have brought a snack to help pass the time.

It was a waiting game, and both sides knew that when the pale green Blazer went away, the waiting Mexicans would swarm across the railroad bridge and make a break onto the streets of downtown El Paso. They would walk, the lucky ones would buy or beg a ride, and the farther they got from the border the better their chances would be of getting to Denver or St. Louis or Chicago and finding work. Hard labor and low pay, but better than they could hope to find at home. With the devaluations and the inflation and the unemployment at home—and we think *we've* got problems—every dollar they could make would be a blessing for some family back on this side of the border.

I shook my head. Here in the quiet and sunshine of the early afternoon, it all looked so tranquil and relaxed. It wasn't. Not for those people sitting over there talking softly among themselves, watching across the river, waiting for the Blazer to go somewhere else to try to catch and deport someone else.

It was odd, I thought, how we could have so much. And appreciate it so little.

I turned and took a side street back toward the touristy strip of gimcrack shops and bars and busy, busy people.

The two men were coming down the sidewalk toward me. I only noticed them at all because there was so little traffic here. A block away there were pedestrians by the thousands, but here there were no storefronts. The squalid, whitewashed buildings had their windows painted over and their doors padlocked. I got the impression that most of the structures were used for storage, probably filled with the stuff that was sold so eagerly to the tourists.

So I noticed the men but paid little attention to them. When they got closer, they looked vaguely familiar.

And angry.

I had no idea what they might have had to be angry about, unless it was a simple matter of accumulated frustrations.

Anyone can find a thousand reasons to feel frustrated these days. An unemployed young male in Mexico might be able to find more reasons than most. It's a shame, but it's also a fact. Just the way things are.

Whatever the reasons—and, hell, maybe I've been giving them entirely too much credit; maybe they were just a pair of creeps who liked to hurt people or mug them—these two stopped a few yards in front of me.

They grinned at me, but they managed to do it without seeming the least bit friendly.

One of them said something to me in Spanish.

I cocked my head and looked at them more closely. By now I had stopped too. There was only a matter of feet between us.

"Sorry," I told them, "I don't speak the language."

The one on the right spoke again. I think he repeated what he had said before, but I wouldn't swear to that.

"Say now, I think I do know you boys," I said. "This morning, right? In that bar?" I grinned back at them. "Sure. You're the boys that were staring at my lady friend."

The one on the left turned and said something to his partner.

So much, I thought, for my belief that tourists can't be molested in border towns. Not likely to be, maybe. But it ain't entirely impossible.

I grinned bigger. A really trusting soul, now—somebody who's convinced that he, or she, has all the answers on human nature—would realize that all Mexicans are meek and humble and polite and probably would conclude that these two lads had stopped me to inquire about the time or something.

Personally, I've known a fair number of Hispanics, and I've pretty much concluded that they can be just as good or just as bad as anybody else. Hell, I might even go so far as to conclude that they are normal human beings. And like with any other of the so-called ethnic groupings, I've decided that I prefer to form my opinions about them one person at a time.

With these particular boys I was about to conclude that I would not want to trust them a whole helluva lot.

The one on the right took a few steps around to the side, kind of slipping around ready for an escape attempt, while his buddy reached into his pocket.

I sighed and hoped the fellow was reaching for a Kleenex.

He pulled out one of those long, gaudy, cheaply made switchblades that they peddle on the streets down here. Cheap construction, maybe, but the thing snapped open with a touch of the button and locked into place with a very solid-sounding *clunk*.

I turned a little and took a step backward so my back was toward the peeling stucco wall of one of the empty buildings on this block.

Psychology, I told myself. That'll do it. I smiled at them and shook my head. See? No threat from this ol' gringo. That sort of thing is the same regardless of language. No threat, no fuss. You don't bother me and I won't bother you.

The one with the knife said something to his partner, who seemed to be unarmed—maybe the poor fellas were needy souls; like, after drinking up all their ready cash they now needed some financial assistance from me so they could afford to buy the other guy a switchblade of his own—and both of them closed the pincers, moving in on me with what sure looked like a fair degree of practice.

So much for psychology and the soothing effects of nonviolence.

They really should have inquired first. Politely. This just didn't happen to be a day when I felt like being mugged.

Before they could get around to the rest of their act I let my face crumble into a mask of stark terror. I let out a high-pitched squeak and doubled over.

Nobody is scared of a terrified wimp. I didn't have to look straight at them to see the tension ease. Their posture lost that rigid, wire-tight stance of impending combat, and the one with the knife took a step forward. All they had to do now was take or do whatever it was they wanted. Right?

I swiveled to my left, still bent over and cowering, and snapped the toe of my boot straight into the blademan's nuts.

Very efficient, the pointy toe of a cowperson-type boot. The guy went kinda pale behind his mustache. He squealed, somewhat louder than I had just been able to manage and with much more feeling, and it was his turn to double over. The switchblade hit the pavement and bounced, and the guy didn't seem real concerned about scratching the imitation mother-of-pearl handle.

The other guy seemed a bit surprised too. He had time for his eyes to go wide and to switch his expression from a glare to a stare. Then I wandered over to him—well, kinda quicker than that might make it sound—and chopped my knuckles straight and hard into the throat cartilage just below his Adam's apple.

Not fancy, or even fair, but reasonably effective. He

doubled over too—it seemed to be a good day for that—and began concentrating on the chore of getting air down into his lungs. From the way he was going at it, I would guess it was a pretty heavy chore to manage.

His buddy, meantime, was down on his knees on the sidewalk puking.

I would have done some other tourist a favor by breaking the blade off his switchblade, but I really didn't want to touch the thing in the condition it was now in, so I left it, and them, where they were and beat a quick retreat around the corner to the safety of the busy main drag just a block away.

I will admit that my knees felt like they were carrying more than the usual load before I made that block, and I was grateful to find a bar on the corner where I could turn in and get a cold Dos Equis.

9

After supper Leah and I took a taxi back across the border. This time her telephone call brought us an invitation to meet Carmen at her home, which was in a thoroughly modern apartment complex on—I think—the southeast side of Juárez. I will admit that the twists and turns of driving in the strange city quite defeated me. I can find my way into or out of any wild and unfamiliar hunk of countryside I've ever seen, but this city driving in Juárez whupped me. I had the excuse that it was after dark, but the truth is that I don't think that would have made a lick of difference. The cabbie could have been taking us by way of Disneyland and I wouldn't have know the difference.

Once we were there, the apartment house could as easily have been in Colorado Springs as Juárez. It was modern-anonymous on the outside and modern-homey on the inside. There would have been no way to tell just from appearances which side of the border we were on.

Carmen was younger than I would have expected, somehow. Younger-looking, anyway. She had to have some maturity because she had at least one grown son, but she didn't look old enough. I'd have guessed her age at early thirties.

She was trim and attractive and very pleasant. She said she was a bookkeeper for one of the retail stores in Juárez, and I'd have been willing to bet that she was quite competent at it. Another stereotypical expectation shattered.

When we arrived she was alone in the apartment. She said her husband worked evenings several nights each week, and the children had been sent off to a friend's home. She offered us coffee or tea and some delectable little sugar-covered cookies, and I made like a mouse while Leah brought Carmen up-to-date on Stella's welfare. After a little while there was a knock on the door, and a very nice-looking couple joined us.

The man had the kind of physical appearance that would have made him a winner as a politician. Handsomely middle-aged and turning silver at the temples. Tailored suit of some silky gray material. He had the kind of rugged good looks that reminded me of Gilbert Roland.

The young woman with him was probably twenty years his junior and was neatly but not as elegantly dressed. Her clothing fit her so well because of her youthful figure, and she was not wearing any jewelry. It took only a matter of seconds for their attitudes and awarenesses to show that they were together but were not a couple. The man gave Carmen a friendly hug hello while the young woman held back, looking shy.

They were introduced to us as Raoul Martinez and Inez something-or-other. Martinez's English was passable—a lot better than my Spanish will ever be—and Inez said so little that I had no idea about her linguistic abilities.

"Raoul is my employer," Carmen explained. "He helped Julio make contact with the coyote who was to take him across that time. Inez was with them that night."

Martinez smiled and shook hands with a formal little half-bow. "Actually," he said, "it is unclear which of us is of greater benefit to the other. My business could not be run without the help of my Carmencita. Without her loyalty to me, poof, she would be overwhelmed by businessmen trying to hire her."

Carmen accepted the compliments gracefully but with obvious pleasure. She got us all seated in the small living room and did the obligatory social bit with cups and glasses and trays.

"You're a businessman here, Mr. Martinez?" I asked.

"I have that pleasure, Señor Heller."

"But you helped Julio find a coyote."

"I did."

"Why?"

"It is simple, Señor Heller. I am a fortunate man. This was not always so. My family did not have wealth. When I was young, I too was a wetback." He smiled. "I see that this surprises you."

"Yes, sir, it does."

"I am an intelligent man, Señor Heller. Please. Do not misunderstand me. I do not say this to, I believe you say, brag. It is a fact. No more. I learned long ago that intelligence will not fill an empty belly. Not alone.

"I also learned that there is more opportunity for advancement on your side of the border. So that is where I went. A coyote took me across the border, señor. The fee then was small by the standards of today. It was enormous by my standards at the time.

"The coyote took me across with fourteen other young men very much like me. We were contracted to work picking crops in your state of Washington. I had agreed to pick fruit as a migrant worker for one year. At the end of that time I left. I found work as a janitor, then as a stock clerk, finally as a salesman. All of this in a store in Memphis. I learned. I saved my money. When I could I returned here and began my own business. I have done well enough. I would not have done so well if I had not been a wetback in your country, señor Heller. Now when a friend asks for my help, I cannot refuse it." He shook his head. "But it is my hope, Señor, that my aid has not brought harm to my Carmencita's Julio. That would be heavy to bear."

I nodded. "What about you, Inez? Carmen said you were with Julio when he crossed?"

From her expression I guessed that she understood what I was asking, or thought she did, but was not entirely sure she was getting it correctly. She turned and said something to Carmen, and the two of them spoke in Spanish for a moment.

"If you do not mind?" Carmen asked.

"Of course not."

With frequent pauses to listen and to translate, Carmen said, "Inez was one of eight who tried to cross that night. Julio was also with them. And of course the coyote. They drove by van to the east, along the river, after dark. She does not know how far they went. Some distance away from the cities.

"The coyote parked the van, and they walked north. She does not know how far."

Inez's voice, although I couldn't understand her, was soft and shy and liquid. The tone was more that of a girl than a woman. She was pleasant to listen to in the intervals.

"They crossed a wire fence and then another. In the brush past the second fence she heard much shouting, and she was very frightened. Men with guns, bandits, stopped them and demanded their money. Inez had very little. One of the men and then the other . . . caused her an unpleasantness . . . in the sight of the others."

Carmen looked uncomfortable translating that part, and I guessed the choice of wording was hers rather than Inez's. I couldn't blame her. Rape isn't something you talk much about with strangers. "There were two bandits?" I asked.

Carmen repeated it in Spanish. "Yes."

"Sorry for the interruption. Go ahead, please."

"Yes." She and Inez talked back and forth for a moment.

"When the bandits went away they went on to the river. It was close then and had not much water. They all took their shoes away. Excuse me. They took their shoes off and carried them. They waded through the water.

"There was not so much brush on the other side. They put their shoes back on. She remembers that Julio was in the front of the group, near the coyote.

"One of the men saw something. A reflection, she

thinks. It was *la migra*. One of their cars. They all hid, but there was not much to hide behind. *La migra* saw them, and two cars of them came. She said they were very loud and had the electric things . . . bullhorns? . . . and told them to stop. Some of the men ran, and *la migra* chased them. One *chota* stayed behind. Inez heard the coyote whisper for everyone to be quiet. She says she was very frightened. She was . . . sore and did not think she could run very fast. She heard a movement where the coyote was and then nothing. *La migra* came very near but did not see them. After a time he went away.

"When the coyote said they could stand, there were only the coyote and Inez and one other man there. Later they found two other men hiding in the field. Those men said they saw *la migra* catch someone, but they did not know who or how many.

"Inez thought Julio had hidden near the coyote. She does not remember seeing him after that. He might have run. He may have been caught. He may have gotten away and not been seen again. She does not know." Carmen sighed and took a sip of iced tea.

"What about Inez?" I asked. "How did she come to be back here?"

After some consultation Carmen said, "Inez was taken in a, uh, motor home to Atlanta. She was given work putting dresses onto dolls and packing the dolls into boxes. She was there only a few days. Then *la migra* came. There were twenty-two illegals there. They were put onto a bus with others and sent back here." Carmen shrugged. "Now she is trying to find money to go back."

"Would she go again with the same coyote?"

Carmen asked. She looked disapproving when she said, "She says that she would. The work was good and she was not treated badly by the coyote."

My opinion . . . well, nobody had asked my opinion. To Martinez I asked, "Would you mind telling me about this coyote, sir?"

"If this would help." He hesitated. "May I speak freely?"

"Of course."

"I have heard perhaps more of this story than you, señor. I think I would not send anyone to this man again."

"Why is that, sir?"

"It is my impression, señor, that the coyote did too little to protect. And I suspect that Julio may indeed have hidden beside the coyote. The girl said she heard a rattling in the brush where the coyote was. Carmencita told you she heard movement." He turned to Carmen. "Would 'rattle' also be accurate?"

She thought that over for a moment. "Yes."

"I believe, señor, the coyote may have been afraid Julio was going to make a noise to bring *la migra*. I think it is possible that the coyote killed Julio himself to stop the boy from making the noise."

I thought about that for a bit. "It could be. It might also be that Julio ran with that first bunch and got lost. Anything might have happened to him, anything from a rancher's watchdogs to being hit on the highway."

"That is possible, señor," Martinez agreed.

"But you don't believe that, do you, sir?"

"No."

Carmen had started to cry. I kept forgetting that this was a member of her family we were discussing here. Talking about the various ways the kid could have been offed was probably not the most considerate thing we could have done.

"I think," I said, "I need to get to know this coyote. Does he speak English?"

Both Martinez and Carmen looked surprised by the question.

"You did not know, señor?"

"Know what?"

"A coyote must travel freely on both sides of the border. Nearly all are Americans."

10

I lay awake trying to force some ideas to come. Leah was beside me, her breathing deep and steady. I could feel the warmth of her against my hip. She kept the big, dark hotel room from being the empty, lonely place it could have been.

I sighed and reached for the ashtray and my cigarettes and lighter. The flare of the propane flame competed briefly with the streetlights filtering through the curtains and then the room was dark again. As dark as you were likely to get in a city. For a moment I missed the starlit silence of my home.

The problem was to get close to the son of a bitch.

He called himself Duke, but Martinez said he did not know the coyote's real name. He was supposed to be a plump, blond, happy-looking man. Martinez said he was not very good with American accents, but he did not think the man was a Texan. I smiled a little into the night remembering how careful Raoul had been to avoid the word *gringo*. A couple of times it had almost gotten the better of him and come near to slipping out. Not that I would have cared, particularly, but I appreciated the man's trying to avoid offense. I've been called a whole lot worse than that.

Thinking about Martinez and his manners, though, was just a way to avoid the problem. Which was that I really was not sure where to go from here.

I saw a Charles Bronson movie once where he was a Border Patrol officer trying to run down a coyote. He went over and passed as a wetback himself. I wouldn't have been a bit too proud to borrow that same idea, except that I look about as gringo as you can get. If that's a right way to put it. Even if it isn't, I still look like a sure-enough gringo, and there would be no bloody way I could pretend to be anything but what I am.

So scratch that notion. Pity. It would have been kinda interesting.

I thought about that and about simpler schemes . . . like being downright direct. I could always kidnap this guy Duke and beat on him until he decided we should have a long talk.

The problem with that one—aside from the fact that I'm not all that convinced of the alleged incompetence of the Mexican police—is that I really didn't know yet if Duke had done anything to harm Julio.

I mean, there is something essentially sleazy about the profession of coyote-ism (wrestle with that one for a while; I think I've come up with a new word), but there are those who could also look at it as a way one person can help another to survive. Personal opinions aside, I just don't figure I've got the right to go around strong-arming people. Let yourself go to thinking that way and pretty soon you have to conclude that the end justifies the means and all that crap. And if I ever got to thinking that, and none of my neighbors had the good sense to put me out of my misery, I'd just have to let my hair grow and begin quoting Marx.

No, thanks, I concluded. I have enough faults and carry enough guilts without going out and deliberately adding to the load.

I smoked another smoke and thought some about Charles Bronson—he sure seems to be one tough son of a buck—and eased out of bed to go sit in the john and contemplate.

While I was sitting there, not particularly enjoying yet another nocturnal cigarette, my thoughts did some flipping and twisting, and I commenced to grin.

Come morning I sent Leah off on a shopping spree and went to have a few words with Raoul.

11

The bar was fairly busy at this late-afternoon time of day and much noisier than was comfortable. I'd been here three days in a row now, and you would think I'd be getting used to it. I wasn't.

As I had each day before, I ordered a Dos Equis and laid my money down. The waitress brought it out cold and still capped and used an old-fashioned church key to pry off the top, right there before my very eyes. Maybe some tourists are so scared of being ripped off that they think even the beers are substituted for cheaper brands. That might be paranoia or it might have some basis in fact, I wouldn't know. Certainly it wouldn't have occurred to me if the joint didn't have that strange habit about the bottle opening.

The girl set down my beer, took my money, and left. That was one nice thing about the place. Whatever the waitresses might or might not choose to do, they weren't pushy about anything here.

That was about the *only* good thing I'd found about the bar. That and the fact that their beer was kept cold.

It was noisy and dirty and got more and more crowded as the afternoon wore into evening. The jukebox held a mixed bag of brassy Mexican music and gut-thumping gringo rock. As far as I could determine, there wasn't a good selection available; if there was, I hadn't yet heard it played. Everything I'd heard there so far had been both loud and obnoxious. Someone sure liked it, though, because the machine was working all the time.

I was sitting at the same table I'd been occupying right along, off to the side and well out of the mainstream of traffic. For the past couple days I had sat there for four hours or so, drinking slowly and not trying to strike up any conversations. There were a number of others in the place who seemed to be regulars. They generally had their own preferred tables, and some of them seemed to know one another pretty well. I avoided them, and they left me alone.

I was about halfway through my second beer of the afternoon when this greasy-haired punk in a skin-tight muscle shirt came slinking in the front door. He had something sticking out of his back pocket that might have been a comb handle. When he reached back and pulled it out, though, the dang thing was a cosh, one of those leather-and-lead billies like some cops overuse.

The punk was creeping up behind a plump, happy-looking fellow sitting at the next table.

"Hey!"

I came off my chair just as the punk raised his cosh ready to bean the guy.

I grabbed his wrist, and we wrestled some until he dropped the innocent-looking but highly effective weapon. He eeled out of my grasp and beat it at high speed out the front door and away before I could lay hands on him again.

I bent to pick up the sap, tossed it onto the table in front of the guy who had almost been bashed, and went back to my beer.

"Say, mister, what was that all about?" His voice had a good old midwestern twang to it. Missouri, I guessed, or maybe Iowa. Someplace, anyhow, where they grow corn and let the cow plops squish up between their toes in the summer.

I shrugged and took a swallow of the beer. It really isn't bad stuff, if a bit heavier than my favored Coors.

There was a fairly sizable crowd around the man now, most of them talking in rapidfire Spanish that he seemed to understand perfectly well. He talked to them for several minutes, and I was willing to bet that the story got more hair-raising with each fresh account. After a bit he came over and stood on the other side of my table facing me.

"Excuse me?"

"Yes?"

"I owe you some thanks, friend. Could I buy you a beer?"

I smiled at him. "You bet. Have a seat and drink one with me if you want."

The pudgy-looking man—I took a second look and decided he was built wide more than he was actually plump—took a chair and shoved his hand forward. We shook.

"Duke Braxton," he said.

"Carl Heller."

"It's my pleasure, Carl. Say, did that young fellow give any idea of what he was mad about?"

I thought about that for a moment, then shook my head. "I can't remember hearing him say a word, Duke."

"That sure bothers me. I don't like having folks mad at me. 'Specially when I don't know what for." He shrugged.

"Robbery?" I asked. "Naw, not in here."

"No, that isn't likely." Duke looked at me for a moment. "You're able to handle yourself all right, Carl. I . . . stop me if I'm out of line . . . but I have good ears. I listen to things, you know. A few days ago I heard some beaners—real street toughs, if you know the type—talking about some guy they'd tried to take down. The description coulda fit you, Carl."

I smiled. "My description could fit a lot of guys. And anyway it wasn't any big deal. The guy with the knife ought to learn not to get so confident just because he has some steel to hide behind."

Duke chuckled. "Not that you're saying it was you."

"You're right, Duke, I don't believe I did say anything like that." I took another swallow from the brown bottle.

"You've been in here the past couple of days, I noticed."

I shrugged. "Nothing better to do."

"Are you here visiting?"

"Aw, it might turn out that way. I don't know. I'm at loose ends, sort of. Got laid off back home in Denver. Didn't have anything holding me there and no prospects that I heard of. I just kinda drifted down this way to see if I could find a way to make a buck. You know."

Duke nodded. "Forgive me for being so nosy, but what's your line, Carl?"

"Oh, I've done a little of this, some of that—ranch hand, lineman for the rural electric, single-unit truck drivin'—you know how it is. My last job I was driving delivery for an auto-parts outfit. That's the one I got laid off from. I expect I can handle just about anything that goes over the road except maybe some of the eighteen-wheelers. The shift's awful different on them, I guess."

"You can handle yourself too, right?"

I grinned at him. "Mostly. But only a damn fool claims he can come out on top every time."

"Myself, Carl, I'm too fat and out of condition for that kind of thing. I'm the kind that comes out on the *bottom* every time."

I squinted and took my time about looking him over. Then I grinned some more. "I'll tell you what, Duke. You can fool some of the people all of the time, and all that stuff. But if I was ever to have to tangle with you, well, I think I'd want some assistance. Like maybe a two-by-four upside the head. Real sudden, too, before you'd know it was coming. You dress fat an' even talk fat, but there ain't much of the real article on you. And I'm betting the same's true when you say you're out of shape. Nosir, Duke, this here is one of those times when you can't fool quite all of the people."

Duke chuckled and sat up straighter. He seemed to approve of my calling him a liar. Or maybe he just didn't look at it quite that way. "What kind of work is it you're looking for, Carl?"

"Anything that gets me to the end of that rainbow everybody's always talking about, my man."

"Anything?"

I shrugged. "I'm sure there's lines would have to be drawn someplace. But I'm not real fussy."

"Listen, Carl, I don't have to work tonight, and I sure could use some company when I go out looking for a good time. Want to come along?"

"You bet."

We finished the beers Duke had ordered and left the place. Since I'd taken a taxi over, Duke drove. I wasn't particularly surprised to discover that the man was driving a van.

It was an interesting evening and in other company it likely would have been fun. As it was I had to settle for interesting. Cheap, too. Duke insisted on paying for everything. The man did not seem to have a problem with cash flow.

When he finally dropped me off at a cab stand—I insisted on it, although he tried to drive me back to my hotel, unspecified as to which one—I took a few minutes more despite the late hour and gave Raoul a call.

Martinez was pleased. And he said his young friend had thought a hundred bucks was more than enough for a few minutes of play-acting like a young punk with a sap. If there was anything more he could do to help . . .

I whistled up a cab and whistled my way back to the del Norte and Leah's waiting arms.

12

It had been an interesting evening and it turned into an interesting—for lack of any other halfway suitable word—relationship. For several nights running I met Duke over on the Mexican side of the border and spent the evening in his company.

I'd more or less expected the guy to be a braggart and a womanizer, but at least as far as I could see he wasn't either one of those. He talked a little, about nothing particularly interesting, and he drank steadily. He never seemed to be drunk or anything close to it.

From time to time, regardless of what bar or joint we happened to be in at that moment, Duke would be approached by one or as many as four Mexicans, mostly but not exclusively male, and they would speak in Spanish. I couldn't make out diddly-flip from those conversations except for an occasional use of *la migra* and *peso*. Duke Braxton, at least as far as my Yankified ears could peg it, seemed to speak the language with nativelike efficiency.

Whatever they were talking about—and I had my suspicions—he never made any apologies or explanations to me.

Several times, though, I recognized the same fellows coming over to have a word with the coyote, and I guessed that he had some subcontractors on staff to help him line up his pigeons for the crossings.

Not that it was supposed to be any of my never-mind. I smiled and nodded and then looked the other way while I sipped my suds and pretended to have no interest in their conversations. Well . . . pretense wasn't really necessary there since I hadn't the foggiest what they were talking about anyhow.

All in all it wasn't too awful. Duke kept right on picking up the tab for everything. And during the rest of the time there was Leah.

The lady was still quite a gal.

She did get a little hacked with me once, though.

We were having dinner, lunch if you prefer, at a steak house over on the El Paso side, where I was insisting she stay lately. I didn't want the complications that could come from running into Duke or one of his pals over on the Juárez side.

Anyway, we were sitting there minding our own sirloins, and this other couple came in and were seated at the next table. I mean, we were there first and everything. It sure wasn't *my* fault that the hostess put them at the table. And I was already facing in that direction.

Perfect innocence is what I'm claiming here, and it's true.

They were a young couple, call it early to mid-twenties, and the fellow was a good-looking youngster in a three-piece suit and mustache. He had that upwardly mobile junior-exec look.

His companion was pretty obviously not his wife. Or anyone's.

She had that look about her. Blond hair worn long and loose and full in a carryover of the Farrah Fawcett style, and she was pretty if not quite up to raving quality. The types who go in for ratings systems would likely give her an eight or possibly a nine, and her meticulously applied makeup was doing its level best to try and bring her up to the ten category.

Her figure I couldn't say much about, as she was wearing a lightweight raincoat even though it was warm and dry outside, or had been the last I'd looked.

And I'll swear that I wasn't really interested in looking to see what kind of figure the darn woman had.

I mean, I was there with Leah, right? It wasn't like I was either lacking or looking. I was hog happy with what I had at the moment. And this total female stranger was there with a fellow of her very own too. It wasn't like she was stalking the place alone with a hungry look in her eye or anything.

So they sit down and order drinks—margueritas, if it makes any difference—and I'm sitting there with Leah enjoying the company and the steak and the baked and that was that, right? Wrong.

After a bit my eye happens to catch the fact that this raincoat across the way is unbuttoned. And kinda sliding apart. And exposing this very nicely shaped knee.

No big deal. And it wasn't like I was staring or anything. The gal just happened to be sitting straight in front of me, that's all. And having the usual mix of male hormones, I simply happened to notice it. I went back to eating steak and talking.

After a bit longer, well, I couldn't help but notice that the coat had slipped just a little farther open.

Very nice lower thighs, too. There was no way I could've avoided noticing. Silky sheen of ultrasheer pantyhose. Fine packaging.

So this time maybe I looked deliberately. The calves were just as nice over a set of teeter-totter high heels that looked plumb dangerous for actual wear but which sure set off a leg.

By now maybe I was paying some actual attention. Not that my blood pressure was up or anything, but, hell, there it was.

Every forward motion for the marguerita glass seemed to make that coat slide just a wee bit more apart.

And every little bit of that exposed just a wee bit more of that nicely formed, nicely textured thigh.

And I will admit that I was beginning to wonder just what the hell this girl was wearing underneath that raincoat.

Another three inches and the V-shaped gap of tan fabric would reach what the boys used to call "possible," and there hadn't been any sign yet of a skirt or hem or any darn thing except nylon and flesh.

So maybe my attention had been drawn by this time. Couldn't help it.

"Carl."

"Mmmm?" I came back to the real world and looked into the soft, gold-brown of Leah's eyes. Very pretty eyes. Very lovely lady.

"I just asked you a question."

"Sorry. My mind was wandering."

"Oh." She smiled. Then she frowned. A little. She turned and took a look, and I guess it was pretty obvious where my attention had gotten off to. "Oh," she repeated. She frowned again.

It seemed pointless trying to deny the obvious, so I put on a sheepish, little-boy grin. That didn't do me any more good than a denial would have, but at least it was honest. I should have gotten some points for that.

I worked *real* hard at keeping my eyes pointed within the space our own table provided after that, and now it was

Leah who kept slipping glances sideways toward the girl with the raincoat.

By then—okay, so I wasn't a hundred percent successful about trying to keep my eyes at our table—things across the way were getting fairly steamy.

Still no visible evidence that the young lady was dressed for anything more street-suitable than flashing, and now she was playing with the rising young exec's leg.

I have no idea how far they might have gone—kinks seem to be in for some folks these days—but about the fourth or fifth time Leah looked over that way—by now I think she was just as curious as I was about what was or was not going to be hidden—the girl caught Leah looking.

They had this very brief but rather complete exchange of glances, then the coat was primly pulled closed.

The girl leaned forward and whispered something into her companion's ear. Whatever it was—and I somehow doubt that it had anything to do with what had just been happening—the guy seemed right happy to settle for half a drink as his lunch. He threw a bill onto the table, and the two of them were gone within seconds. I didn't feel sorry for him. Somehow I doubt that that change of plans ruined his day. In fact, I suspect just the opposite could be true.

We watched them leave, and after a moment I just couldn't help grinning.

Leah tried to look stern and unforgiving, but what the hell. After a moment or two she was laughing.

"A cocktail waitress," I speculated.

Leah looked at her watch. "She goes on duty in half an hour."

"Plenty of time," I assured her.

We both got to laughing.

Damned if the woman didn't throw that up to me for *days* afterwards, though.

Anytime she got the tiniest bit miffed with me after that, she'd bring up unkind—and totally unwarranted—remarks about my tongue hanging out and neck swelling and stuff. And I *swear* I was innocent. I never hardly noticed. Hardly.

13

"You're all right, Carl."

I raised my glass toward him in a silent salute. "Thankee, Duke. You're okay too."

"I . . ." He was interrupted by the appearance at his side of a slender Mexican woman of thirty or so who would have been pretty except for an unfortunate pattern of pockmarks on her cheeks. She squatted low beside Duke and spoke to him in soft, quick Spanish. Her tone of voice was definitely pleading. I didn't need to understand the words to follow that. After a few minutes Duke shook his head and said something to her, and she went away.

I watched her go. I was feeling sorry for her, but Duke couldn't have known that.

"You like that?" he asked with what sounded like genuine curiosity.

I shrugged.

"If you want some I could arrange it."

I shook my head.

"You don't like girls?"

I grinned at him. "Disease, my man. It runs rampant. I'm not so damned macho that herpes can't scare the fool out of me."

Duke chuckled. "I really do like you, Carl."

I raised my glass and saluted him again.

"Have you, uh, lined up any prospects since you got here?"

"Nothing serious. I had something in mind, but it fell through."

"That's a shame."

"Ain't that the truth. If something doesn't spring soon, I might have to go look for honest work."

Duke chuckled some more. He turned and waved for a couple more drinks even though these weren't hardly dented yet. When he turned back to me he said, "I might have an idea that could do you some good, Carl."

"Shoot."

Duke grinned. "How'd you guess."

"What?"

"Nothing. A joke, that's all. Tell me, Carl. What do you know about illegals? Wetbacks?"

I shrugged. "Not much except that there's a lot of them. See 'em by the bridge all the time. See 'em running from the law on the other side. Read in the papers what a nuisance they are." I grinned. "According to a couple congressmen I've read about, wetbacks are the biggest reason our economy's in the crapper. Other than the usual, though, I couldn't say that I know much about them."

"You got anything against them?"

I shrugged. "Never had any reason to think about them either way when it comes to that."

Duke nodded. He seemed satisfied by the answer.

"Why?"

"A man can make a lot of money nursemaiding wets, Carl."

"You're woofing me, right?"

"Not at all. A lot of money."

I tried to look skeptical. "I don't know, Duke. All these poor bastards I've seen down by the bridge, they don't look like they've got ten pesos to the herd of 'em."

"The ones down by the bridge don't. That bridge is strictly last resort. That's for the ones that can't afford to pay a coyote for a safe trip over and a job on this side waiting for them. For that, Carl, whole families'll pool their funds together, just to get one of them earning a decent income."

"Coyote," I said. "I've heard the word, but I don't remember where. Except for the prairie-wolf kind, of course."

He explained what it meant and added, "There's some who would call me a coyote, Carl. Personally, I prefer to think of it as providing people with opportunities."

"I'll be damned. Is that what . . . ?" I waved in the general direction where the Mexican woman had disappeared a few minutes before.

"Uh-huh. That particular one, though, she didn't have the fee. She thought she could work off the rest of it. You get some like that." He grinned. "Sometimes it's even worth it."

I gave the scuz a wink and a leer to let him know I was just as low a character as he was.

"Have you ever thought about work like that, Carl?"

"I couldn't honestly tell you that I have, Duke. Hell, I don't know that much about the business. But I couldn't say that I'd mind it if the money was right."

"What I had in mind, Carl, wasn't any kind of partnership. You ought to know that right up front. But the money could be real right for you, and you might be able to do something for me at the same time as I'm doing something for you. You know what I mean?"

"Tell me."

What Duke had in mind, in many many words, was a sort of on-the-job training program in how to be a coyote. He said he could show me how and where to get wets across the border. Whenever I was ready I could set up in business for myself, moving them just across the river and a few miles into Texas. Then he would take them over for delivery to the industrial areas across the U.S. where cheap labor is in demand.

"As it is right now, Carl, I'm having to take on the whole damn load of work on this thing. Crossings and delivery too. I'd still want to have my own crossing operation. There's good money in that. But the money's just as good—and safer—at the other end. Don't get me wrong. I'm not offering to split commissions with you from the employer's side of it. That stays mine. But I've got more demand for workers that I can fill by myself down here. The wets I bring across, I charge whatever I want and keep all of it. The wets you deliver to me, you charge them whatever you can get and it's yours. Like I said, it could work out to benefit the both of us. You'd make out all right with just the fees the beaners pay."

I looked doubtful again. "Just what is it you call 'all right,' Duke?"

He shrugged. "Say you bring over ten of them at five hundred a head. That's five thou for a night's work, Carl."

I whistled long and low. "Five hundred just for wading across a lousy river?"

"That's modest if there's a guaranteed job attached to it, Carl. And by feeding them to me, you can offer that. Like I said, I've got more jobs than wets. Hell, Carl, five hundred's easy. Colombians, Nicaraguans, they'll pay a couple thousand. Even after you pay for trucks and drivers a man should clear six or seven thousand a week."

I gave him another whistle.

"Does it sound good?"

"Is the Pope Polish? Hell yes, it sounds good. What's the risk?"

Braxton shrugged. "First offense, a few hundred bail. After that, if you're dumb enough to get caught twice, it goes up. The operating expenses more or less depend on how good a lawyer you get and how much the bastard gouges you. There's nothing that I'd call a serious risk. It sure as hell beats drugs when it comes to risk weighed against reward, I'll tell you that."

Damned if it didn't seem to at that. I told him so.

"So tell me, Carl. Do you want to get your feet wet?"

I thought about it for a moment. "I might could stand it, Duke."

Braxton grinned. He looked at his watch and tossed off the rest of his drink. "Timing, Carl. That's real important." He stood up. "Coming?"

"Tonight?"

"A man can't earn a living sitting on his butt."

I left the rest of my drink and stood. "Lead the way, my man. I'm always willing to learn something new."

14

We drove east in Braxton's van. He guided the boxy vehicle with the easy assurance of someone who was familiar with the route, someone who knew where he was going. Duke pointed out street signs and landmarks as we went, but I knew it would take me a few runs over this same territory to become comfortable with the strange surroundings. I really don't know if it was the fact that we were indeed in another country that was short-circuiting my usual sense of direction or if it was the particular enterprise we were engaged in that was bothering me.

Duke stopped finally at a bus stop where half-a-dozen people were waiting. It seemed an odd time of night for so many to be waiting for a bus, assuming there was public transportation available at that late hour, but of course it was Duke they were waiting for.

Over the next fifteen minutes or so another half-dozen people arrived in taxis and private cars to be deposited into the back of the van. The twelve people, ten men and two women, made a tight-packed load back there. When everyone was in—and Duke's fees collected, in cash that he carefully counted before the person was allowed into the van—Duke drove east away from town.

It was too dark for me to see what the country was like

around us, but I didn't really have to. It would be dry and drab and thorny, just like on the other side of the alleged river—sand strip was more like it—that was the international boundary. Immediately alongside the course of the river it would be brushy and in some places wooded, but those twin, semigreen strips along either side of the Rio were only a matter of yards deep.

We passed through several small towns, villages really, and stopped beside a perfectly ordinary barbed-wire fence.

"Did you notice that little rock cairn beside the road back there?" Duke asked.

I nodded.

"We're two-tenths past it. Remember that. There's some other markers on ahead. I put 'em there myself. The path is always two-tenths of a mile past my marker. That marker is the first of seven. I number them in the order you come to them, so if I agree to meet you at number five, say, you just start off from the fifth cairn and my rigs will be waiting at the other end."

"Sounds simple enough."

"*La migra* knows about all of them, of course, but there's a helluva lot of territory for them to cover out here, and my groups sure hell aren't the only ones trying to cross in this area."

"I thought they had all sorts of detection gear out along the border."

Duke grinned. "Not near as much as you might think. Over in Southern Cal they have a lot more 'cause there's a lot more traffic coming through over there. Wets and drugs both. They spend a lot of money and manpower over there. It isn't so bad around here as they'd like people to believe."

I nodded. And hoped the guy knew what he was talking

about. A lockup is not my idea of a keen way to end an evening.

Duke unloaded the Mexicans, a nervously excited group whose expressions kept shifting between eagerness and fear, and gave them some sort of long lecture in Spanish. "Telling them to shut up and stay together," he said for my benefit. "We go single file, and if we're hit by bandits we stick together regardless. If *la migra* jumps us, then it's every man for himself and to jail with the hindmost."

"Are there likely to be bandits?"

Braxton shrugged. "Sometimes. It's easy pickings for them. The policy is to not fight. Remember that, Carl. They'll leave the coyote alone, for obvious reasons—don't wanta kill the goose that delivers their golden eggs and all that."

"What about the wets?"

Another shrug. "Long as they're quiet and do what they're told there's no trouble."

"If there is trouble?"

"Don't you mix into it, Carl. Never. Leave them be and you can keep a good thing going. Whatever else happens, you never get into it."

"I'm told wets can get killed trying to cross."

"Same as you and me, Carl, they could get killed trying to cross the damn street. Just don't mix in whenever you're jumped. I mean that."

The man's concern for human life was monumental, I could tell. A real humanitarian. Maybe, I thought, there were some coyotes around who really did care about the welfare of the people they were allegedly trying to help. It was a nice thought, however improbable.

"Come on," Duke said, "we have to get started." He spoke to the wets and formed them into a tight line, then told me, "You stick with me, Carl. If *la migra* shows, stay on me, whatever happens."

"Or bandits," I added.

"Exactly."

The night was warm and clear, the stars extraordinarily bright overhead. I could see the light-glow of El Paso and Juárez to the west, but there was no moon overhead. I suspected that that was a deliberate decision on Braxton's part when he chose the crossing dates, and reminded myself to ask him later.

There was some confusion when we wriggled through the barbed-wire fence. Most of the party acted like it was something they hadn't done very often before, and it led to some nervous laughter. Braxton, I noticed, seemed to expect that and let them get it out of their systems before he reminded them they were supposed to be silent.

Then, Braxton in the lead and me close behind him, we set off through some Mexican rancher's pasture toward the north.

Duke seemed to know where he was going quite well. The light was poor, and though he was carrying a flashlight he never needed to turn it on. He followed a footpath that I could feel much better than I could see, and he set a brisk pace. Behind me I could hear a few whispers and some heavy breathing.

We came to a second fence line after about three-quarters of a mile. The expected brush was just beyond it. This time Duke cautioned the wets against noise before they crossed the wire, and this time they did it without the laughter.

"Very close now," he told me, then said something, presumably the same message, in Spanish to his charges.

We walked at a much slower pace through a thorny alley that had been hacked or worn in the midst of the tall growth around us, and after only minutes broke out onto the edge of the sand strip with a trickle of water running down the middle. Duke paused there to listen for some time before he seemed satisfied. He held a finger to his lips, turned, and dog-trotted down onto the flat sand.

Following him, I felt vulnerable and exposed. The cream-red sand that was so ordinary by day was a place of danger by night. Out here there was no place to hide. Little opportunity to run if someone should be waiting on the other side.

We splashed—rather noisily—through the strand of sluggishly flowing shallow water and continued to trot across the equally wide and dangerous piece of exposed sand on the U.S. side.

Back home, I thought. Whoopee! It occurred to me that if we were grabbed over here I was a criminal. It was not a delightful thought.

Thank goodness we reached the brush line again without incident. Most of the wets—illegal aliens now, technically speaking—were gasping and wheezing. Duke stopped and gave everyone time to get some breath back. He looked at me and grinned. "Piece of cake, eh?" he whispered.

"Piece of cake," I agreed.

After five minutes or so we walked on out. There was no fence on this side, and I noticed that Braxton moved at a much slower pace here. He stopped every few minutes to listen and look, obviously alert for signs of *la migra* lurking somewhere in the darkness. There was nothing to alarm him.

We walked a mile, maybe a mile and a quarter, and found a twin-tracked path. Duke turned left along it and after another few minutes reached the looming bulk of a U-Haul truck that was waiting for us. It was a single-unit rig of about eighteen feet, fully enclosed. The driver was dozing behind the wheel. There were some mattresses, an ice chest, and some grocery bags in the back end.

Braxton said something in Spanish and accepted a round of handshakes and grins before the new wets began crawling into the back of the truck. When they were all inside, the driver closed and padlocked the cargo door, gave Braxton a wave, and went off about his business.

"Where are they going?" I couldn't help asking it.

"Chicago for this bunch," Duke said.

"All the way in the back of that thing?"

He shook his head. "Trucks have to be checked for weight and loading every time they cross a state line. They'll unload in Monahans—that's right along the interstate route, much safer to travel since you don't call attention to yourself—and transfer to another van." He grinned. "The long-hauler has the name of a church choir on the side and some fake luggage in the rack up top. Once they're in that, they're as good as delivered."

I chuckled and snorted and slapped him on the shoulder to hide my reaction. Deception, particularly against authority, usually tickles me. I can get a kick out of a really clever con man. For some reason, this pissed me off.

Duke stood there listening for a while. After five minutes or so he said, "I haven't heard anything, and that's good. The first few miles are the most dangerous. Once they're on the hard road they should be all right, and once they reach the interstate they're loose and running." He sounded pleased with himself. "Ready?"

"Where to?"

"Back to the van, of course."

"You cross back over every time?"

"Hell yes, Carl. Think about it. They see me crossing

over here all the time. What goes over legally has to come back the same way or they'll get suspicious." He laughed. "That's one of the advantages of being a fat man, Carl. They know me pretty well at the border by now. Dumb bastards think I'm coming over and staying late at a whorehouse. I roll my eyes and rub my crotch, and they think I've been over there having a helluva time." He smiled. "And of course I have been."

"You think of everything, don't you, Duke?"

"Damn straight, Carl. And don't you worry. You're going to do just fine."

We turned and walked back toward Mexico. I suppose we were about to commit another crime when we crossed the border going in that direction, but it hardly seemed important.

Somewhere to the north of us, the wets in their padlocked cage were riding through Texas. I hoped it would all go well for them.

15

Raoul joined Leah and me for breakfast at the hotel. He was there already when we got down to the restaurant and already had orange juice and rolls waiting, along with an insulated carafe of coffee. He looked prosperous and distinguished and genuinely pleased to see us.

I couldn't help thinking that this was one of the imponderables. Raoul was smiling and pleasant and Mexican, and I'm sure it was entirely legal that he should be sitting in an El Paso hotel coffee shop waiting for us. Yet, just a few hours earlier I had been in the company of other Mexican citizens, on our side of the international border, who were literally risking their lives to cross into the country.

When we were done with our meal Raoul would tell us goodbye and go on about his business, on either side of the border that the press of business required, and no one would think a thing about it.

Appropriate? Sure. But why was it normal and acceptable for him to come over here but such a big smelly deal for some poor peon from Sinaloa to make the same crossing? Raoul contributed to our economy by doing some of his wholesale buying over here, I understood. But the ragtag fruit picker from Sinaloa contributed to it with his labor. Somehow I couldn't find a whole lot of reasons for differentiating between the two kinds of contributions. I guess that is something that only wiser heads than mine can comprehend.

Anyway, Raoul seemed pleased to see us and relieved as well. "Your adventure of the night was safely concluded, Carl?"

"How did you know about it?" I hadn't known myself that we were going across until I was with Duke the night before. I couldn't have told Raoul about it if I'd wanted to.

Raoul smiled and spread his hands. "There are few things that are not seen, my friend. El coyote's van is well known, and you were seen in his company. I made the assumption that you remained with him."

"You assumed correctly then," I admitted.

"You had no troubles?"

"None."

"You were fortunate."

I shrugged.

"If there were no robberies and no deaths, you were fortunate."

"It was a cakewalk." Raoul looked puzzled. "No trouble," I amended.

"I wish you wouldn't talk about robberies and deaths," Leah said with a shiver of distaste. "I'm frightened enough for this knothead," she pointed my way, "without that." She made sure the friendly insult would not be misinterpreted by laying her hand on my wrist with an affectionate possessiveness.

"My apologies," Raoul said. To me he added, "Please do be careful, though, my friend. Go cautiously and well armed always."

"Cautious, you bet," I agreed, "but borders and firearms make me nervous. I don't really want to be carrying back and forth." I had been leaving my Smith in a suitcase rather than risk crossing a border check with it. I understand it can get real exciting if they find you with a pistol in your pocket. And those boys in the customs shed are said to have no sense of humor whatsoever.

The attitude seemed perfectly logical to me, but Raoul looked plumb upset. "But, Carl, you must *not* go out there unarmed."

I explained my feelings on the subject again, this time in somewhat greater detail.

"I understand, my friend, but . . ." Raoul thought for a few moments. "Would you accept my help with this thing?"

I shrugged.

"I could arrange something for you perhaps. An availability, so to speak. The article in question would not have to cross back and forth with you."

Leah shook her head. She looked at me. "I don't like that idea, Carl. People get hurt when they carry guns."

"Honey," I told her, "people get hurt when other people want to hurt them. The point of having a gun is to keep them from doing that whenever they want to."

"I don't like it," she said.

"I know, but it might not be a bad idea. Just in case." To Raoul I said, "If it wouldn't be too much trouble, I'll take you up on your offer."

He thought a moment, then gave me the name of a soft-drink vendor whose cart could nearly always be found near the Juárez end of the downtown bridge. "He will have the package for you anytime you ask for it," Raoul said. "Return it to him and he will keep it for you until you ask for it again."

It seemed okay—very helpful, even—except for the minor point that I don't always like other people to know what I'm doing at any particular moment. I didn't want to make a big point of it with Raoul—it could have seemed awfully ungracious of me after all the trouble he was willing to go to to be helpful—but I kind of decided to pick up the offered package and then figure out some sort of hidey-hole over on the Mexican side that wouldn't require using the unknown quantity of a street vendor for storage and retrieval.

And, hell, after the smooth way things had gone last night, I really didn't think I would be needing any kind of armament for the short time it should take to get something on Duke Braxton. It was just that I would feel somewhat better knowing I wasn't defenseless in the unlikely event that I should need something to make loud noises with.

I thanked Raoul, and we finished our meal with Leah sitting there unnaturally quiet between us. I figured that as soon as Raoul left we could go back up to the room, and I could spend the rest of the morning taking Leah's mind off the serious side of things.

That prospect did not displease me.

16

Leah wanted to spend the afternoon by herself. She made it pretty clear that she did not want me along. My first thought was that, generous and thoughtful as she was, she wanted to slip away and buy me a present or something, and I was going to try to dissuade her. Then I realized that this was not something pleasant she had in mind. A tightness around her eyes and a faint undertone in her voice said that this was no kind of cheerful thing she was planning, although she was trying to hide that from me.

I did a little cussing at myself then. I'd gotten so intent on Duke Braxton and my own problems that I had very nearly forgotten the kind of pain Leah must have been in all this time. She had become pretty good at hiding that, or else she had learned to simply accept the amounts of agony that bled through the protective barrier of the painkillers she took several times each day.

And she had mentioned that there was some "miracle

cure" crap she wanted to check out down here on the border.

Not that I had any hopes for her in that area. I doubt that she could have had any herself. McQueen's death—man, he was a motorcycling fella first class—had done a lot to rip away the false hopes in apricot pits and mescaline and all that junk. Though I'm still not sure if maybe the false hopes were better than no hopes at all.

Anyway, Leah hadn't hardly mentioned her physical problems since we'd gotten there. I don't doubt at all that she was protecting me from it. If she needed some time alone now to do whatever it was she considered necessary, well, she was damn sure entitled to it.

I wanted to take her in my arms and make it all better. But I couldn't. So I held her very close and kissed her and faked a smile when I told her goodbye. That romp on the big, rumpled bed could wait until another time.

The hotel room seemed too big and too empty without her, and daytime television has darn little to offer, so I locked up almost as soon as Leah had had time to clear the lobby and took the elevator down.

I wasn't in any humor for solitary drinking, so I drifted out into the bright glare of the dry, El Paso heat and wandered idly along the littered street to the international bridge.

Still on the El Paso side I passed and ignored a pair of streetwalkers of the weird persuasion. One of them was wearing a fake leopard-spotted tunic and had tiger stripes dyed in her equally fake blond hair. She also—I swear it—had cat's whiskers painted on her face. This was on the U.S. side, for crying out loud. In spite of all the crapola you hear about border towns, the streets seemed a whole lot safer for family touristing on the Juárez side than on this strip between the Paso del Norte and the bridge. An observation like that can almost destroy a man's faith in stereotypes.

Down by the bridge there was a Border Patrol vehicle in evidence again, a pale green Bronco this time, and across the river I could see the loiterers waiting, hoping *la migra* would go away so they could cross. I couldn't see the two Patrol officers in the Bronco, but I could see the backs of their heads turning occasionally and bobbing in conversation. I wondered if they ever felt like two small sandbags trying to hold back a flood. I joined the flow of humanity on the walkway leading south.

On the Juárez side of the bridge I was engulfed once again by the busy, loud, cheerful mob of shoppers and sellers. The place has an almost carnival atmosphere.

I bought a square of excessively sweet praline from one vendor and a cut-rate carton of cigarettes from another. The boys who swarm the streets selling U.S. brands of cigarettes at North Carolina prices are almost invariably young and lean and eager and friendly. In Denver you'd expect a teenager out trying to scrape a living on his own to be sulky and resentful that the manna wasn't falling into his lap, but these kids didn't act at all like that, and I liked them.

Come to think of it, though, I'm not being fair about that. Up home in the cities you can find plenty of kids about that same age making it by selling bunches of flowers at cut rates on the streetcorners, and those kids seem to have that same happy attitude toward life and customers as these Mexican boys did. So maybe it is the fact of their working, making it without manna, that keeps the sulks out of their expressions regardless of which side of the border they happen to live on.

I had to laugh at myself just a bit then. If there is anyone alive who is *not* qualified to espouse the work ethic it would have to be Carl Heller. A devotion to gainful employment is hardly something I've ever been noted for. A lot of other things, but not that.

I killed some time shopping in the little cubbyhole stores that lined the street and managed to find a pair of earrings for Leah that should perfectly accent the necklace I had given her before. I knew she would like them and had the added satisfaction of knowing I would be able to give her a present when she didn't have an exchange gift picked out for me. . . . I'm not above that kind of selfishness, time to time.

The steerhorn chair I had admired before was still there, or one enough like it that I couldn't see any difference. I gave some serious thought to buying the hideous thing, then thought about buying it and having it shipped to Leah instead of back home to the ranch. But it seemed like a lot of money for a very poor joke, so I contented myself with a few chuckles at the thought and let it go at that. No need to embarrass the poor woman by taking unfair advantage of her politeness. If I sent the damn thing she would feel obligated to put it someplace in her house, and that would have been going a bit too far. The gentleman running the shop looked somewhat puzzled when I walked out of his store snickering. You see, I'd come up with the perfect alternative to buying it and sending it to Leah. Instead of buying it, I'd simply tell her that I had done it.

I wandered on down the street in absolutely no hurry.

Leah still wasn't back at the hotel when I checked in there late in the afternoon, and I had told Braxton I'd meet him for supper, so I left her a note and went back across the border.

A taxi took me to the specified restaurant. Turned out to

be a total waste of the fare. I had been walking back and forth in front of the place all afternoon without ever once noticing its name.

Unlike the place where Carmen had intended to meet us, this was a tourist-trade sort of place with cutesy-quaint decorations dripping from every available surface and a menu that was big on such standard American goodies as tacos and burritos.

Braxton was already there when I arrived. He had a beer at his elbow and an impatient look on his face every time he surveyed the menu. He also seemed pleased to see me. We shook hands and almost in the same motion he was waving a waiter to the table.

"How goes it, Carl?"

"Fine, you?"

"In a minute." He went back to his study of the menu and gave a long order in fluent Spanish. I asked for the enchilada platter—I love the things back home, so why not here too?—and a beer to wash it down with.

"Now," Duke said when the important stuff was done with, "what do you think of our little experience last night?" He was grinning.

I grinned back at him. "Easy livin', my man. If it's always that smooth, you ought to be ashamed of yourself for taking the fees."

Duke chuckled. "I won't say it's always that easy, Carl, but that gives you a good idea of the way it can be. But what do you think? Really now."

"Hell, I liked it."

"Good." Duke reached into a pocket and pulled out a wad of folded green. He tossed it onto the placemat in front of me.

"What's this?"

"You don't recognize it?"

"So what's it for?"

"For you, Carl. Three hundred. For last night."

"Hell, Duke, I didn't do anything but go along for a walk with you. You don't owe me anything."

"You were there, weren't you? You were ready to help any way you could, right? Take it."

I hesitated. But only for a moment. As an out-of-work guy on the make for big bucks, I wouldn't be expected to turn down free money. I picked up the wad and stuck it into my pocket without counting it. "Thanks."

Duke waved the thank-you aside. "It's nothing, Carl, compared to what's still to come. If you're with me, that is."

"Count on it."

Duke grinned. "I was hoping you'd say that. I tell you, Carl, with you running a source of supply for me at this end, I can double my up-north sales. This is gonna work out just fine for the both of us."

The waiter brought our meal. The enchiladas were as good as I had hoped they might be. Duke had enchiladas, tamales, a plate of nachos loaded with black olives and guacamole, and another side plate of tacos. Appaently the guy ate as much like a fat man as he looked like one. He was also highly serious about his eating. The conversation was at a standstill until he was done.

"Do you think you could handle yourself after one more walk-through with me?" he asked over a refill on the beers.

"I think so."

"You *think* so?"

"No sweat," I assured him.

"Okay. Come over with me one more time. Day after

tomorrow. After that I'll set you up with some contacts to find your wets and a driver to haul for you on this side. Unless you have a truck or van of your own, that is. Naturally I'll be taking care of the pickup on the other side. You set your own fees and pay your help yourself, okay?"

"It sounds more than fair to me, Duke."

"Good. I brought some things for you to read." He reached under his chair and put a paper bag on the table for me. I took a look inside. They turned out to be Border Patrol training manuals. "All public-record stuff, Carl. Perfectly legal."

I grinned at him.

"Meantime, I have to make some calls to Chicago. Make sure everything's lined up. I'll be busy the next few days, so I'll meet you the day after tomorrow. Nine P.M. be all right with you?"

"Whatever you say."

"Nine o'clock then. At the cockroach."

I got the name of the bar without him having to translate it for me. "All right. Good luck to you in the meantime." We shook hands, and Duke took off with a gracefully fluid motion that seemed odd for a man his size.

It wasn't until he was gone, disappearing quickly into the crowd on the sidewalk, that I realized the bill had been left for me to pay.

I pulled out the wad Duke had given me and used some of it to pay the rather hefty-for-two tab.

17

There were a lot more wets waiting to cross this time, a total of nineteen who showed up at the same bus stop right at ten o'clock. Duke packed most of them into a shiny new single-unit truck with some Spanish words—I couldn't begin to tell you what it might have said—and a painting of a huge chicken on the aluminum sidewalls. It probably would have been reasonable to guess that the truck belonged to a company that sold either eggs or friers. It could possibly have belonged to a fraternal organization for cowards. Whatever, most of the wets went into the truck, and the overflow was put into Braxton's van. He had me ride in the truck cab with the driver, a young man who spoke passable English but who had rather little to say.

We followed the same route east out of Juárez, and this time I was able to anticipate most of the turns. I didn't feel nearly as lost and confused as I had the first time we came this way.

I only hoped the rest of the night would go as smoothly as that first crossing had been.

The van passed the first rock cairn and two-tenths of a mile farther the brake lights flared. Route 1 to points north, I thought. Same old stuff.

The barbed-wire fence and the breezeless silence of the

night were the way I remembered them too. The stars overhead were dimmed, turned into fuzzily faint impressions of light, by a thin, high overcast that had either moved in recently or was so light I had failed to notice it before.

Duke stood beside the door of his van for several moments before he let the wets unload. He stood with his head lifted and eyes closed. I'm sure he was listening for any foreign sounds in the night, but I swear it looked like his nostrils were flaring too. He might well have been sniffing the air for predators' scents, from the impression he gave.

Finally he nodded. He motioned toward the driver of the truck, whose name was Roberto, and waved for me to join him.

"We don't want to take too many in a group," Duke said. "Too much noise, you know. Ten is usually the max, maybe a few more, but of course you can decide that for yourself. Anyway, what I like to do is split 'em when I have a lot. Think you can follow me with a second group tonight, Carl?"

"Sure. I've been on the path before. No problem."

Duke nodded. "Like I told you the last time, if you have any trouble you just stand quiet if it's on this side. Run like hell if it's on the other. If there's bandits, don't worry about it and don't cause no trouble. If it's *la migra,* I'll make sure there's enough noise to warn you and you can cut out." He smiled. "Right?"

"Easy," I said.

He clapped me on the shoulder. "Good enough."

Roberto already had the wets from both vehicles assembled into a single group. Braxton walked into the center of them, arbitrarily dividing them into two groups of ten and nine men each. There were no women crossing this time. I was finally getting bright enough to realize that this probably had a lot more to do with the demands of Braxton's northern industrial employer/customers than with the supply of willing wetbacks waiting to cross.

Braxton said something to the wets, then gave the truck driver a nod. Roberto climbed back into his shiny new, chicken pluckin' truck and drove away back toward the lights of Juárez. Even with the van still sitting there, the countryside seemed emptier and much more lonely with the big truck gone.

Duke began to address the wets in Spanish. Obviously some last-minute instructions and cautions. I didn't really have to understand the words to know more or less what was being said.

"Carl," he said after a few minutes. He motioned me closer. I stood beside him and he draped an arm across my shoulders while he continued to talk to the wets. I felt kind of like a counselor being introduced to the kids on the first day of summer camp.

Still, with the cold bulk of a much-worn Browning .380 in my jeans pockets, this was hardly the time or place to be reminded of summer camps. Things could get just a bit more serious here.

Thinking about the gun, I let my hand brush lightly over the pocket to reassure myself that the Browning was where it was supposed to be. It was.

It had also been where it was supposed to be, available immediately and without comment when I'd asked for it earlier in the evening. The vendor had handed it over in a paper bag, fully loaded with copperclads and with a loaded spare magazine as well. Raoul had been as good as his word, and I reminded myself that I should use some of

Braxton's money to repay Raoul for the gun and for the trouble he had gone to to get it to me.

Duke finished his spiel to the wets and told me, "This group on the right is yours, Carl." I smiled and nodded to them and got a round of nervous smiles in return. "You won't have to tell them anything that you can't do with sign language. I've already told them to keep their mouths shut at all times and to go wherever you lead them. You shoudn't have any problems."

"All right."

"We'll be moving slow, so give me a ten-minute start, then come ahead. I'll be waiting for you at the rig on the other side. Remember, now. If there's bandits, freeze. If you see *la migra,* leave your wets and run back here to the van. Wait for me here if that happens."

I nodded.

Duke grinned. "See you later, amigo."

"Ciao." Hell, I'm acquainted with other languages too. One word at a time maybe, but . . .

Braxton shepherded his group of ten across the road and through the fence. They were out of sight within paces after they'd stepped away from the barbed wire and the reference point of the fence posts.

I looked at my group of wets. They were grinning at me. They looked nervous. Well, if they'd known my lack of experience, they'd have been a whole lot more nervous. As far as they were concerned, this was a matter quite literally of life and death, and it was my inexpert hands their lives and futures had been entrusted to. No wonder the poor guys looked nervous.

I gave them what I hoped was a reassuring smile and tried to concentrate on my wristwatch. The wets were whispering softly among themselves. I knew they had been told to be silent, but if the sound of the van and the chicken truck hadn't alerted anyone, this little bit of whispering wouldn't hurt for sure.

Given ten minutes to wait, and not being able to speak a word of their language, there was no way I could have avoided looking into the faces of these men who were trusting me.

Aside from seeming justifiably nervous, they all looked . . . hopeful. Very hopeful, very eager. Lordy, how glad they seemed to be to be getting an opportunity to labor and to earn a wage from that work.

I had no idea what that work might be. I could be sure it would be hard and the pay low. They might have had no better an idea than I did about what they would be required to do on the job. I got the impression that it really didn't matter so long as they had *some*thing to do. I felt sorry for them. And pleased for them at the same time. I suppose I should have felt ashamed, this being an entirely illegal undertaking and all. I didn't.

When enough time had passed, I smiled at my charges and crooked a finger. They bunched tightly behind me like so many chicks tucked under a hen's wing, and we crossed the road and fumbled our way quietly through the wire fence. I noticed that this group—possibly because they knew there was no communication possible between us—was much quieter about the indignities and the humor of the awkward wire crossing than the group had been the other night.

I found the path by feel more than sight and walked along it at a fair pace, considering the lack of visibility. I was walking somewhat faster than Duke had led us that other time, but I was comfortable with the rate of travel. And I suspected that I might be a little more comfortable in the woods and the brush than was Mr. Braxton, despite his greater degree of experience on this particular little stretch of soil. Anyway, we made good time, and the wets seemed to be having no trouble at all keeping up with me. They padded right along with an endurance and a silence that would have tickled a Green Beret D.I.

Something—the pitch of the ground, a general impression of deeper black in the blackness of the night ahead, a barely sensed hint of coolness from the denser growth ahead—something warned me that we were coming to the second wire fence ahead, and I slowed our pace to make damn sure I wouldn't suffer the embarrassment of leading a bunch of men smack into barbed wire in the darkness.

I thought I could hear something very faint in front of us, and I stopped. The wets stopped obediently behind me. I turned and held a finger to my lips to remind them, probably unnecessarily, to keep their mouths shut.

Up ahead I could definitely hear something now. I couldn't make out any words, but there was a whole lot of whispering going on up there.

That didn't seem right, and I began to get a bit worried.

We were still on Mexican territory, so it couldn't possibly be a Border Patrol net set up at the fence. At least I didn't think they could come over on this side, regardless of provocation. Certainly there had been no warning sounds from Braxton.

This wasn't in Duke's list of helpful hints and gentle instructions, and I knew that frantic wishing wasn't going to make me learn Spanish in a flash of sudden inspiration. Still, most gestures are universal. I turned and tapped the first man in my group, then pointed to the ground at his feet. Sort of a sit-stay command for humans. He looked puzzled for the briefest of moments, then nodded. He turned and repeated the gestures to the guy behind him, and they started passing it on down the line. I made one final stay-put gesture toward the first guy in line, then dropped into a crouch and began to skinny forward along the path.

I had been right. We were close to the second fence. When I got there—wishing for some burnt cork to black my face—the last of Duke's people were being allowed through the fence.

I say "allowed through" because there were some strangers among them. Three men, as best I could make out. One of them was standing chin to chin with Braxton, and I wasn't sure but I thought that one had something in his hand. Possibly a pistol. Not that Duke was doing any resisting. He was following his own advice and standing like a gentleman while his wets were delivered.

The other two strangers were in the last stages of relieving Braxton's wets of their burdens. At least those burdens like cash, watches, jewelry, what-have-you.

One guy was riding herd on the group while the third member of this nasty trio shook down the wets one at a time. He had them empty their pockets, then patted them down thoroughly for money belts, looked inside their socks and shoes, and like that. Very efficient and very well practiced, I thought. While he worked he kept mumbling something—threats or warnings, probably—in Spanish. His voice was more growl than whisper. I could hear it clearly enough, and I didn't like it.

Most of Duke's group was already on the other side of the wire, stripped of whatever few valuables they might have possessed. I got the impression that the coyote's warnings had been followed and they had offered no resistance.

The next to the last man, though, still on this side of the barbed wire, said something to the bandit when the fellow went to frisk him. The bandito replied with the kind of snarl that did not really require interpretation.

The wet turned his own pockets inside out and handed the bandit something. He was wearing sandals, so there was no need to search him down low, but the bandit did it anyway and checked him as well for a money belt, which the fellow did not have. Then the bandit reached out to snatch something—I couldn't see what—from around the wet's neck.

The wet must have been full up with either beer or machismo, because he took a step backward and snapped something at the bandit, some brief comment in Spanish that sounded sharp and nasty even to my untutored Anglo ears.

I winced as the bandit's hand flashed in the darkness, and the hard steel of a pistol barrel slashed across the wet's face. I could hear the moist, dull impact across the distance that separated us, and the wet staggered and almost went to his knees.

The Browning was in my hand almost before I knew I intended to pull it, but *damn* it could do no good for the poor bastard over there. Shooting a strange gun, particularly a pocket model that isn't very accurate even if you know the weapon, and shooting it at night at uncertain targets, well, that is only a way to prove you're an ass. If I'd made the mistake of firing, I would have had just as much a chance of hitting the wet as the bandit, and regardless of what else happened I would probably be only making things worse for everyone. Not only allowing this robbery to take place—which it already had—but destroying these people's chance to get to the other side as well.

I put the damn pistol back into my pocket and gritted my teeth as the bandit's hand moved again and the wet got another pistol-whipping.

Duke said something to the bandit in a pacifying tone of voice, and the man lowered his arm.

The bandit grunted out something ugly-sounding and reached up to snatch the whatever-it-was from the wet's neck. There was no resistance to him this time. I wondered what it was that was so important to the poor bastard that he would take a thrashing to try to preserve it. A pouch of cash? Probably nothing more valuable than a treasured locket or charm. But that bastard of a bandito just *had* to have it.

The bandit growled at the man again, and the fellow stood weak-kneed and swaying until the last wet had been stripped of his goodies and was free to help the injured wet on across the fence.

Duke was released to join them, and the three bandits stood in arrogant confidence while the now totally impoverished bunch of wets under Duke's command disappeared into the darkness along the path. It took only seconds for the bunch to move beyond my vision, although they were moving slowly now. The man who had been pistol-whipped had to lean on two of the others to make it.

Bastards, I thought.

The three bandits didn't bother to go anywhere to try to hide. On a night this dark they didn't have to. They just sank down into the low growth around them and were safely hidden. Simple motionlessness was quite enough to hide them now. And for sure if I hadn't gotten this advance warning I would have led my group right into them.

Feeling a little uneasy in my stomach after the unnecessary violence of that third bandit, I turned and slithered back the way I had come.

My group was still exactly where I had left them. If any of them had so much as wiggled an ear while I was gone I couldn't tell it. Certainly I hadn't heard them.

They did look relieved, though, when I slipped out of the shadows to join them. Probably they had been waiting there, wondering if they had been brought just this far and then dumped, still on the Mexican side of the border. Hell, coyotes are not noted for their humanitarianism. It was the sort of thing I would have feared if I had been left like that. I wished all over again that I had the ability to speak to them, to offer the reassurances when necessary and the explanations they deserved. There just wasn't any way.

I looked at them and wished I could tell them what was going on. The thing was, these men were my responsibility now, and the way I saw it, it was my job to get them over the line *safely*. Not just safe from *la migra* but safe from those creeps that were still waiting up ahead to pluck them and send them on as poor and as defenseless as possible. I sighed a little bit and felt more of a weight of responsibility than I had really wanted here.

"Does anybody here speak English?" I whispered.

They stared back at me with all the responsive understanding of a litter of pups.

"Thanks a lot, Duke," I muttered under my breath.

I took the precaution of motioning for silence again, then took the first man's right hand and hooked it into the back of my waistband. I mimed for him to do the same to the next man in line. Within seconds we were all hooked together like that. We might not speak the same language, but they weren't stupid. I looked once again to make sure we were all hooked together—I sure didn't want anyone to get separated from the group in the dark, away from the path where I would have to take them—and led off.

Getting around the waiting ambush was simple enough, if damnably slow.

We couldn't move very fast without breaking brush and

making noise, but it wasn't much of a trick to walk a counted three hundred paces west before we crossed the fence and made our way slowly—and painfully; those thorns were sharp enough to sew with—through the brush to the river. Then turn and go another counted three hundred paces downstream.

The opening of the path coming out of the brush on the Mexican side was right where it was supposed to be. I smiled a little, let the wets unhook themselves from one another, and we wandered through the sand and the warm, shallow water to the U.S. side.

My wets' grins told me they knew where they were now.

From there it was strictly routine getting them out to the waiting trucks, a pair of gaudy yellow Ryders this time, and on their way to wherever they were bound.

Duke was waiting there as he'd said. He looked pleased with the night's work even though his people had been ripped off.

"Any trouble?" he asked in a normal tone of voice. I had sort of been tuned to a whisper, and the sound seemed loud in the night.

"Not a bit," I assured him.

"We got hit by the banditos."

The trucks fired up and pulled away.

"So I saw," I told him. "I heard the commotion up ahead, so I went around them. Like I said, no trouble at all."

Duke grunted. It was the kind of noncommittal sound that could have meant anything, and I wasn't sure if he was pleased that I had gotten past the bandits or upset that I'd chanced leaving the path.

Whatever he was thinking, he didn't discuss it but let the whole thing drop.

"Come on, Carl. It's my treat for the beer when we get back to Juárez." He clapped me on the shoulder, and we headed back across the river toward the van.

I didn't see any sign of the bandits when we reached the fence walking down from the north, but I knew that didn't necessarily mean anything. It was the poor slobs coming from the south they were waiting to hit. Duke had mentioned something about them not bothering the coyotes, a Thieves' Code or some such. Obviously this extended to coyotes walking alone through the night.

Or maybe the bastards had simply taken their new wealth and gone off to spend it.

Whatever, we saw no sign of them, and Duke was as good as his word. He paid for the refreshments when we got back to civilization and slipped me another three hundred dollars besides.

A real decent fella, I thought.

18

The timing could have been worse. We were lying there sweat-sheened and spent, relaxing in the afterglow of something almighty fine—at least I was; I can't swear to exactly what Leah was feeling, but it seemed a pretty safe guess from the languid, purring sounds that she kept making as she snuggled into the curve of my arm—when the bedside phone rang.

"You get it," Leah mumbled. I could feel her lips move against sensitized flesh and could feel the tiny exhalations that came out with the words.

"I don't think I can move yet."

She raised up enough to give me a flash of self-satisfied grin and a brief flick of her tongue in the ear. My half-pained, half-leering response seemed to satisfy. She was giggling when she rolled over to answer the telephone.

"I told you it was for you." She hefted the instrument across to me and set it on my chest.

"Yeah?"

"Carl."

I recognized the voice. "Yes, Raoul."

"Have I disturbed you?"

"Not at all." Well, he hadn't, in a way. And I certainly wasn't going to go into particulars with the man, no matter how nice and helpful he had been.

"Good." He sounded like he didn't believe me, but what the hell. "It is lunchtime, yes?"

"Darned if I know." My watch was all the way over on the chest of drawers. Besides, I didn't really care what time it was.

"Accept my word for this. It is lunchtime."

"Okay."

"As it happens, my friend, I am again on your side of the border for the business. Would you and your lady join me?" He laughed. "For a brunch, perhaps, instead of the hamburger."

I had been enjoying Leah's company and really didn't want to see anyone else at the moment. I would have declined except that I remembered I still owed the guy for the Browning that was now waiting in a hidey-hole over on the other side. "Just a minute, Raoul." I covered the mouthpiece of the phone and asked Leah. Her response was a shrug.

"Sure, Raoul. Where can we meet you?" Leah, the rascal, was wearing nothing but an impish grin and was doing her level best to distract my attention with certain, uh, slurpy manipulations. She was doing a darn good job of it, too. I made a face at her and crossed my eyes, which sent her into another fit of giggling, but I didn't get so rash as to push her away.

"I'm calling from a courtesy telephone in your lobby," Raoul said.

"Give us a few minutes to tidy up and we'll be right down."

"Very good."

Leah disengaged with a rather loud, moist *plop* and pouted at me. I hung up the phone.

"Egad, woman, he probably heard that."

She giggled.

"You ain't got no shame, woman," I told her with a sigh.

"You're right," she said cheerfully. "But I guess I got my orders." She bounded off the bed with a display of energy that amazed me and began throwing clothes on. I shook my head and joined her, somewhat more slowly.

We were downstairs and more or less presentable in under twenty minutes, and much of that time had been spent while I dragged a Bic across the jaw. The woman was an amazement.

Raoul was waiting when we got off the elevator. We shook and howdied and let him shepherd us into the dining room.

I noticed that the service was very attentively applied.

Not, I am sure, because of us tourists but in deference to Raoul's impeccable tailoring and grooming. The man really would have been an ace in politics with his looks and bearing. And it took less than a glance to tell that the man wasn't hurting for cash, either.

Without asking—and I know it was kind of silly of me, but I resented it just a bit—Raoul ordered for all of us. Coffee immediately. Chilled cups of fresh fruit. Steak and eggs for Leah and me with whole-wheat toast and home fries. A petit filet with asparagus spears and Spanish rice for Raoul. No consultation with the menu required.

Like I said, I thought that was just a bit presumptuous of him. Worse, though, the man had gone and ordered *exactly* the right things. It sounded perfectly marvelous, and I was as hungry as a sow bear in February.

"So, Carl," Raoul said when the waitress was done writing in her pad and batting her lashes, "I understand our friend made another little journey last night. Were you with him?"

"Uh-huh."

Raoul nodded. "You seem to be all right. Bueno. All went well, I therefore believe?"

"Well enough." I told him about it. Leah had already heard the story once—there'd been no way we were going to get to sleep without her fears and frets being assuaged—but she got big-eyed and concerned in all the same places again.

Raoul seemed as worried as Leah when I got to the part about the bandits. "You must be more careful, Carl. I already feel responsible for what happened to young Julio. I do not wish to bear the guilt for your harm also."

"Nothing happened, Raoul. Really."

"Not so, my friend. You must understand that a coyote,

which you are certainly pretending to be, would be easy prey for these banditos if they did not expect to shear his flock on other nights. You must not anger them, Carl."

I felt more than mildly exasperated. I knew good and well that Raoul was expressing a genuine concern for my safety. But, dammit, I just can't get real sympathetic to the feelings—or the well-being—of a bunch of lousy holdup artists.

"Those flocks of sheep, as you put it, Raoul, deserve better than to get ripped off by a bunch of creeps with big muscles and big guns. I can't help thinking about that too, you know."

"I know." Raoul leaned forward and touched my forearm. "I believe you are a good man, friend Carl. I only ask you to think of your own safety in this thing."

"I am," I said, "*and* the safety of those poor fellows who were depending on me to get them across safely."

Our meal arrived then, and we let the subject drop. Later I asked Raoul what I owed him for the Browning. The man wouldn't set a price, insisting it had been nothing at all and he was glad for an opportunity to be of help, but I gave him the three hundred dollars Duke had passed to me the night before. Raoul took the money but only, I think, to make me feel better about it.

"I feel better knowing Raoul is there to help," Leah said when we were back in our room after the brunch he had insisted on paying for. She held me close and kissed me. "With both of us worrying about you, maybe we can keep you out of trouble, Carl."

"No trouble," I promised her. "I think I've figured out a way to cause some for Duke Braxton, though. Maybe not enough of it, but anyway a partial payment for Julio."

19

Braxton seemed to be in a particularly fine humor when I got there. He had told me to meet him about eight o'clock, but it looked like he had already been there for quite some time ahead of me. The remains of a meal—plates enough for two normal eaters or three lightweights—were spread out around him. He waved me to a chair and shoved the soiled crockery off to the side. "Hola, amigo."

"Whatever that means," I said agreeably. I sat.

"It means I'm damned glad to see you tonight."

"Good."

A dark-haired girl who was dressed like she was ready to leap into a flamenco at any second hustled over to take our drink orders. Both her smile and her attitude were like sunshine on a leash, and I would have to say that I could get real used to the kind of service a fellow got down on this side of the border. The waiters and waitresses and shopkeepers down here acted like they honest-to-Pete wanted to please.

"Not bad, huh?" Duke said when the girl went away.

"Very pretty," I agreed.

Duke laughed. "We can do better than that, Carl." He gave me a wink. He sure seemed in a better mood tonight than I'd ever seen him in before, and I had to wonder what it was about. It didn't take him long to get to it.

"Good news, Carl. I mean, really good."

I lifted an eyebrow and waited for him to go on.

"I have a helluva deal cooking for us, Carl. Really big. And it won't hurt you either."

"In case you're wondering, I'm interested," I said.

"Thought you would be," he said with a grin. "What it is, Carl, I've gotten orders," he leaned forward and lowered his voice a little, "for sixty wets, man. Sixty of them or as close as I can get."

I whistled softly. No wonder the son of a bitch was excited. Between the crossing fees and the employers' payments, Mr. Braxton should come out of that with a downright gaudy wad of currency. I didn't know for sure, of course, but I was willing to bet he could clear a thousand dollars per person, collecting from both ends like he did, and if my guess was anything close to accurate, it would make for a bundle well worth some excitement. "That's a lot of people."

"Damn right it is. We'll lay on a special effort for this one, Carl."

"How will you do it? Three nights in a row or something?"

He shook his head. "One trip."

"All of them at once?"

"You got it."

"I thought you said ten is about as many as you like to take in one bunch because of the noise they make."

"Normally, yes, but this isn't normal. Like I said, this will be a special trip. I figure I can lead off an' you can bring up the rear to make sure we don't lose any of them."

I looked maybe a bit skeptical, and Duke apparently

misunderstood. "Look," he said, "I know I promised to set you up on your own, Carl, but I could really use you on this thing. We can split the crossing money right down the middle. Naturally I keep the whole bite on the other side, and we take the expenses off the top."

I remembered that I was supposed to be broke and greedy and did some figurative chop-licking over the prospects.

"Your share ought to come to about twelve grand, Carl."

I grinned good and big over that.

"So what do you say, my friend?"

"I say I'm ready anytime you say, my man."

"And I say we go tomorrow night, then."

"Damn, you can have that many lined up so quick?"

"Twice that many if we needed them." He laughed. "There's a lot of things in short supply down here, Carl, but wetbacks isn't one of them."

"All right."

"Meantime, Carl, you and me have got some celebrating to do. If you know what I mean." He winked again.

I had a suspicion of what he meant, all right, and my preference would have been to turn the man down. With what he had just told me, there were certain preparations I sure wanted to make.

But if I ran out on him now, right after he had made his grand announcement, Braxton might very well think something funny was up, particularly since I'd already established the habit of partying with him before.

It made no difference at all that I would have much preferred to go back and cuddle with Leah. If I wanted to keep Duke happy and unsuspecting about me, I'd better trail along with him for the duration of the celebrating.

"I'm with you, Duke."

* * *

The place was a real scuz joint. Duke had driven, of course, and I was pretty thoroughly lost after the maze of unlighted streets we had traveled. Not that I particularly cared. This was not the sort of place I would want to find my way back to.

It was a long, low building of adobe construction—the real stuff, not a stucco imitation—that was so dark inside we had to have escorts to find a table without assaulting the other patrons.

I had no idea how many others were in attendance in that audience, but the amount of smoke and heavy breathing around us made it clear we were not the first customers of the night.

The room—much smaller than I would have guessed from the outside appearance—was filled with tiny cocktail tables and chairs.

There were no candles on the tables and no overhead lights in most of the room, which made the brilliant lighting over the central stage area all the more glaring.

That part was darn sure well lighted.

A battery of floods was hung overhead with—I looked—slightly pink gel filters in front of them.

It was the activity on the stage, of course, that had all the customers snorting and snuffling.

The only stage prop that was needed was a bed.

I could have gotten along very nicely without ever seeing the kind of show they were putting on.

When we came in, the stage, and the bed, was occupied by two women.

There was no pretense at artistry or dance or story line. They were just going at each other, making much noise and doing a lot of groaning. They sounded like a pair of pigs having a disagreement. And maybe that wasn't so far off the mark, come to think of it. About them being a pair of pigs, anyhow. I don't think either of them cared enough about what they were doing to agree or disagree.

The G-string-clad girl who led us to our table seemed to know Braxton, and I would have to say that he seemed to be enjoying the show quite thoroughly.

We were put at a table at ringside, so to speak, which was another hint that Duke was well known here. There was enough light bleeding off from the brightly lighted stage for me to see his expressions clearly, and what I saw there made me uncomfortable. His eyes were bright and his swallowing seemed to come hard. I wasn't positive in that tinted light, but I thought his face had colored with excitement. I expected him to start drooling at any moment.

One nice thing about being so close to the stage was the view we had of the "performers." They were only ten feet or so from us.

I say that was a nice thing because in a way it was damned interesting.

On film, with the right lighting and softening filters, this performance might have come across as erotic.

From farther back in this same room it had been fairly disgusting.

But from right up close it was, well, interesting.

What captured my attention was not what they were doing—or pretending to do—to each other.

It was the expressions on their faces.

Both of them looked about as interested in what they were doing as a woman in a laundromat who has forgotten to bring a magazine along.

There was more there than just the boredom, though. Or less, I guess it would be more accurate to say.

Their expressions were . . . vacant. Lifelessly dull. As

if they would not have been interested enough in anything to bring a magazine to a laundromat.

They probably had been heavily powdered and made up when they came on stage, but apparently they had been there for some time now. The heat of the lights and their exertions had them sweating pretty heavily. That and assorted other juices had pretty well washed away their makeup, and both of them looked hard. Hard and old and tired. I couldn't imagine a sane male getting worked up over either of them.

"Isn't this great, Carl?" There was no music accompanying the performance, and Duke had no trouble at all making himself heard.

"I'll tell you a truth, my man," I said, and then I told him one. "I've never seen anything remotely like this."

"Really?"

"Honest."

Braxton looked tickled to pieces. It was obvious that he figured he had just given me a great and wonderful gift.

The women finished their act, if that's what it was supposed to be, with a crescendo of squealing and howling that I suppose represented passion fulfilled.

The audience clapped and shouted, and some of the men threw tips onto the stage. The kind of tips that could be folded and that make no noise when they hit. All that enthusiasm was beyond me, but I joined in the clapping as a matter of form. I refrained from getting in on the money throwing, though.

This was a real classy place. I think I kind of expected some kind of entertainment between bouts. You know. Some jokes. Some strippers. At the very least an emcee. Not here, boy. The women slouched away with their loot clutched in their hands—they had no place else to carry it;

well, no place logical, anyhow—and were replaced by a fresh but equally bored-looking group of three. Two men this time and one woman. The woman's hair was done up in twin ponytails, or puppydog ears I think they might be called, and I'm sure she was supposed to be a teenage innocent. From where we sat it was clear she had been around long enough to pass through her teens several times. One of the men was carrying a cat o' nine tails, but I was relieved when the stageside view revealed the thing to have lashes that were much too light and flexible to be real. They could put on a show with the thing, but the woman wouldn't really be hurt.

I looked around some and realized from the faces, though, that these customers *wanted* the whip to be real. I got the impression that they would want that badly enough to believe that it was so.

Jesus!

"I'm getting all worked up here, Duke. Is this all the action they have here, or can a guy do some participating?" I truly did not want to sit through this coming performance.

Duke laughed happily. "I know what you mean, Carl, but I don't wanta go to the rooms just yet myself. You go ahead, okay?" While he was talking to me his eyes kept shifting sideways to make sure he wasn't missing any of the wonderful action on the stage.

"If I get done before you, or after, I'll take a cab back," I said.

"Yeah, right." He didn't look my way. Instead he kept looking at the stage, but he made some sort of hand signal that brought a nearly naked Mexican girl on the double-quick.

The girl leaned over and seemed to be munching on Braxton's ear while she talked to him.

"It's my buddy here. He needs some attention, darlin'." He was still looking at the stage.

The girl gave a yip of feigned delight and switched her attention to me. She led me away through the maze of tables after I said a goodbye to Duke that I'm not entirely sure he heard.

There was another room beside this one, a waiting room of sorts, filled with various fleshy offerings. "You would like?" the girl asked.

"You'll do fine," I said. I hadn't really looked at her or at any of the others.

She made some happy sounds and led me farther into the building. Back here the hallway smelled of loud perfume and unmasked body odors. It was the kind of place that makes you think about germs, the old Howard Hughes complex, whenever you have to touch anything. The room, with a crummy little bent-wire hook and eye for a lock, was about what you would expect. As soon as we were inside, the girl slipped out of her high-heeled shoes and G-string. There was nothing else she could have taken off unless she shaved.

"Fifty dollars now, please."

I paid her, and she spread out on the excuse for a bed that took up most of the space in the little room. I was reminded somehow of the old-time cribs that I've heard about but which disappeared long before my time.

"Do you speak English?" I asked.

"Yes."

"I have kind of a special request then."

"Special?"

"Uh-huh."

"Special is more, please."

I gave her another fifty, which seemed to satisfy. I got the impression she didn't give a flip what the special request would be as long as I was willing to cough up the extra fifty.

"Yess, swee-tee." Her smile was about as exciting as the expressions of those two women on stage had been passionate. I was awfully glad at that moment that Leah wasn't in the habit of calling me sweetie, because this would have spoiled it.

"What I want you to do," I said, "is roll over on your stomach. That's right. Turn your head to the right, toward the wall there, and close your eyes. Do you have them closed?"

"Yes."

"Hands down at your sides now. Legs together and held very straight. That's fine. Just like that until I tell you otherwise, okay?"

"Okay, swee-tee."

"Right. Don't open your eyes now, and don't move. Don't pay any attention at all to what I'm doing. Nothing."

"Okay."

So much for that. There was no place to sit unless I wanted to wait on the foot of the bed, and I really didn't think I wanted to have any visits from whatever might have been living in the mattress.

I leaned against the wall and stood there thinking about much more interesting things. Mostly I brought up for visual replay in my memory the contours of my ranch, the valleys and the mountainsides and the aspen-choked slopes, and I tried to imagine and to visualize where each head of my cattle might be at that particular moment.

I felt a little better after I'd done that. Felt a little homesick, too.

After fifteen minutes by my watch, I thanked the girl profusely and got the hell out of there. What kind of kicks and kinks she thought I might have been getting during that time I neither know nor care. I just wanted to get a taxi and scurry back to Leah as fast as I could convince the cabbie to motor.

20

The secretary—or receptionist, officer, Girl Scout maybe; whatever she was titled, she was wearing a green uniform—was a pertly attractive young Hispanic girl with short, gleaming hair. I'd have known which side of the border I was on, though, regardless of her choice of clothing. She was pretty but she was also busy, harried, and impatient with the silly requests of citizens and taxpayers. Before she ever said a word I got the feeling I was supposed to apologize for disturbing her oh-so-important workday.

"Yes." It wasn't really a question. Not much of one, anyway.

And perhaps it was just her demeanor and my own reaction of it, but somehow I couldn't help thinking of this bureaucratic (I don't use that as a compliment, by the way) little civil servant as someone who had turned on her own kind.

That is perfectly silly, I know. The fact that she was Hispanic had nothing to do with anything. She was quite obviously a citizen of the United States in the employ of her own nation. But . . .

"I'd like to see the boss, please," I said humbly and politely. Humility and politeness had no visible effect on her.

"Boss?"

I was almost willing to believe she really hadn't ever heard of such a thing. I tried again. "I have no idea what you call them around here, miss. Shop foreman, honcho, the cog that makes all the little wheels turn."

"That would be Major Samuels," she said briskly.

I smiled at her. "Thank you. May I please see Major Samuels?"

"The major is very busy."

"I'm sure he is," I agreed. "After I talk with him he'll probably be a lot busier."

"What is it you want to see him about?"

"If I thought you could help me, miss, I wouldn't have asked to see the major, would I?"

The question was rhetorical, but the sour-lemon face she made—very briefly—told me what her answer would have been had she chosen to give one. To give the girl credit, though, she didn't say anything to that effect. "I'll see if the major has a moment. Wait over there." She pointed. I waited, but there wasn't going to be any "please" tacked onto the instruction. She turned and went away.

I waited over there.

The officious little snit, as I had started thinking of her, was back shortly. "Major Samuels is busy now." Her attention went immediately back to whatever it was she had been doing before I bothered her.

"Miss." I had to repeat it twice before I got her to look up from her labors.

"I told you. . . ."

"I know you did, and I really appreciate your efforts on my behalf." I smiled brightly. "Really I do. And I know the major must be a very busy man. But he is going to miss a wingdinger of a bust if he doesn't take the time to talk to me. Try him again, will you, please?"

She didn't show any enthusiasm but she did get up again, wearily, and trudge with resignation out of sight once more. Poor thing. Such burdens.

This time she beckoned and led me, without conversation, to an office farther back in the rabbit warren. She showed me inside, still without speaking, and marched away.

The man sitting behind the cluttered desk was wearing civilian clothes, but his bearing was military. If he hadn't been in charge of a Border Patrol office I would have taken him for an army colonel in civvies. The carved walnut plaque on the desk read MAJ. J. T. SAMUELS. He stood when I came in.

"Carl Heller," I told him.

"Samuels here." This, obviously, was where the office got its briskness. He extended a hand to shake and gave the impression that he was coming to attention as well.

Samuels was a tall, lean, steely man. Steel-gray hair cut short and kept carefully trimmed. Gray suit and pearly-gray tie carefully knotted. Square, bristly mustache slightly more silver than gray and kept in military trim.

I got no impression at all, though, that this was an act he was staging. His face was tanned and seamed by duty far from office walls. From the rest of him I would have expected his eyes to be gunfighter blue; instead they were a brightly intelligent brown. All in all, the man looked about as soft as the undercarriage of a railroad car. He looked like he could take a lot of pounding and still get the job done.

"You wanted to see me." No question mark attached.

"Yes, sir. I have information about a large crossing of illegals destined for jobs in the Midwest."

"Sit down." He motioned me to a straight-backed armchair and resumed his own seat behind the desk. "What was your name again, sir?"

I told him.

The major looked thoughtful for a moment, then stood. "You will excuse me for a minute, Mr. Heller."

"All right."

He left me there and was gone for less than five minutes. When he came back he leaned back in his swivel chair and steepled his fingers while he looked past them at me. "You say you have information of a planned crossing."

"Yes, sir, I do."

"Tell me about it."

I did, editing out the trivia. Things like my own participation with Duke Braxton earlier.

The major didn't act particularly impressed, which surprised me. "How do you know about this, Mr. Heller?" At last, a genuine question.

"Braxton and I have done some partying together. He wants me to help move them with him."

"I see."

"Correct me if I'm wrong, Major, but you don't act very pleased to be getting this information. I've already told you who is crossing and with how many illegal aliens and when and where. Would you like me to herd them all in here to the station too, so your boys don't have to go out and chase them?"

The implication that he wasn't interested in his duty got to him. He sat ramrod straight in his chair, and the muscles of his jaw quivered. He had good control, though. He didn't spit or snarl even once. I felt rather fortunate that I wasn't under his command about then.

"You invited me to correct you, Mr. Heller. I shall." The control was much better now. He relaxed enough to lean back in the chair and steeple his fingers again. I've been told that that is one of the ways people can raise a psychological barrier and separate themselves from someone else.

"Please do."

"I am quite interested in your information. I have no doubts that a crossing will indeed take place. Possibly a relatively large-scale crossing. Probably somewhere close to the time frame you suggest. My problem now is to determine where that crossing will actually take place."

"I've already told you, Major, where. . . ."

"I heard you. I do not necessarily believe you."

My jaw might have dropped some. I couldn't say. For damn sure I couldn't believe this. I think I said something to that effect.

"Really, Mr. Heller," the major said coldly. "We are not so easily taken in. Your effort is understandable. It would be most convenient to have my personnel lying in wait in one spot while your friends make their crossing elsewhere."

"What kind of stupidity is this, Major, that makes you suspect citizens who come here trying to do their public duty, for cryin' out loud."

The good major actually smiled at that. I wouldn't have been sure he knew how. "Mr. Heller, I have already informed you that we are not taken in quite so easily as you believe possible. The fact of the matter is, your name already appears on our lists of suspected coyotes, to use the colloquial term. You have been seen in the company of a known trafficker in illegal aliens. Any information you might volunteer is likewise suspect, Mr. Heller."

"Hell yes, I've been seen with a known coyote, man. I told you that myself. . . ."

"Please, Mr. Heller. Argument of your alleged innocence will serve no purpose. The question that occurs to me now is whether I should detain you until after this anticipated crossing has taken place or whether I should let you inform your friends that your diversionary plan has failed." He gave me that thin smile again.

I didn't exactly know what to say to that. He was right about one thing, of course. Protestations of innocence are *always* useless.

"I believe," the major said, "that our wisest course of action might be to detain you for further questioning. Until tomorrow morning, perhaps."

He reached for his telephone.

21

Leaping and running was my first inclination, but that hardly seemed like much of a solution to anything. I mean, if they want you, they're going to have you. The question is when, not whether.

"Major."

"Yes?" The telephone was in his hand, but he hadn't done anything with it yet.

"Don't you think you should check me out before you get drastic?"

"I told you, Mr. Heller, we have already observed you, several times, in the company of a known coyote. From my point of view, that seems ample."

"And I told you . . ."

"Really, Mr. Heller. Please." He hooked a finger into the dial of the instrument. You'd think the federal government could afford modern touch-tone dialing equipment, but this thing was the old-fashioned kind. Like the major?

"Why don't you check me out with the sheriff back home," I suggested. "He knows me. He might be able to put a slightly different light on things."

Samuels seemed to find that amusing. He gave me a tight, thin-lipped smile. Sorta reminded me of a wolf. "We do have newspapers and television down here, you know, Mr. Heller. Even here we have read about some of your—how shall I put this?—creative law enforcement back there."

"I don't understand you."

"I believe our information lists your home as some small town in the mountains of Colorado, correct?"

"Uh-huh."

"If my memory serves me, and I believe that it does, there was a great deal of publicity not long ago about local law enforcement in that area. Something about police personnel who chose not to enforce certain laws pertaining to drugs. Correct?"

I nodded. He smiled.

Unfortunately, he was correct. There'd been lots of articles and broadcasts, *60 Minutes* among them I think, about a certain elected sheriff who hadn't thought the marijuana laws were appropriate and refused to enforce them.

Thanks a heap, buddy, I thought now.

"They aren't all like that, you know," I said. It sounded lame even to me.

"Do you suggest, Mr. Heller, that I ask your opinion of the individuals involved then?"

I sighed. The major smiled.

"Look," I said, trying another tack, "I can see how you might not trust some local you don't know. How 'bout a fed, then?"

"Come again?"

"Would you take the word of a federal officer? Or would you assume that ve haf vays of corrupting all of them too?"

"What kind of federal officer, Mr. Heller?"

"FBI?"

He shrugged. He also took his finger out of the phone dial. "If the FBI would vouch for you . . ."

"Hell, none of them's going to *vouch* for me, man. Not likely, since they don't know what I'm doing down here. But there are some of them back home who, um, you might say they've had occasion to become acquainted with me."

"Friendship, Mr. Heller?"

"No. We've just had occasion to bump into each other from time to time."

He nodded. It was pretty obvious that he would trust reputation a helluva lot more than friendship when it came to this kind of inquiry.

I thought about going into some sort of pitch to remind him of his duties, just in case it turned out that I was being straight with him, which I was, and which he didn't for a minute believe. Yet.

But this guy seemed like the kind who would darn well be

aware of his responsibilities without any reminders from the likes of a suspicious character like one Carl Heller. With this one I thought I would do better to keep my mouth shut on that score and let him do his own thinking.

"I might be willing to make a call like that before we detain you, Mr. Heller."

"If I could suggest a name, then . . . ?"

"Please do."

I gave him the name of Ev Robertson in the Colorado Springs office. Robertson doesn't know me exactly. We darn sure aren't pals, and he probably has a lot more questions about me than he would have answers.

On the other hand, it isn't exactly a secret—much as I would prefer for it to be one—about some of the things I've gotten into here and there. My attitudes and inclinations have brushed up against official interests just a little too often for the secret to be as well kept as I would like.

"Would you object to waiting elsewhere while I make the call in private, Mr. Heller?"

"No, sir. Not if you intend to place that call."

"I said that I would," Samuels said stiffly. His tone of voice stated rather clearly that he was one of the my-word-is-bond types and any implied questioning of that would lead to reactions of the nasty sort.

"I'll be glad to wait."

He buzzed for a secretary—a new one, not the chummy Hispanic kid I'd seen before—and had her take me to "room C."

The C, I think, stood for "cell." Or it should have if it didn't. Bare walls, no windows, and one of those doors that locked automatically when an excessively powerful spring pulled it shut. You needed a key to get out again. They did not provide me with said tool.

There was a drab steel table in the center of the little room and two straight-backed steel chairs. A tin can served as an ashtray. It was the only accessory piece provided to lighten the decor.

Since there was nothing to read, not even a label on the tin can, I fired up a smoke and made myself busy by cleaning out the useless junk from my wallet. Funny how many scraps of trash wind up there no matter how often you weed them out, addresses and telephone numbers that no amount of memory jogging will make meaningful, outdated hunting licenses, stuff like that. I felt pounds lighter when I was done.

I also felt bored. And maybe a wee bit worried. Time was slipping away here, and I had much better things to do than sit around wondering if I was going to be arrested.

It didn't help a whole lot when I got around to remembering that, good intentions or no, if they really wanted to arrest me, they'd have more than sufficient cause if only they knew the particular facts that I hadn't volunteered to them.

After all, I had already played coyote twice myself. Duke Braxton didn't exactly have an exclusive on that around here.

22

We had enough transportation to start a parade. There was Braxton's van, the truck with the chicken painted on the side, a really battered and nasty-looking VW microbus, and a red and white Travelall, one of those stretched versions with lots of seating capacity. Each of the vehicles was stuffed with humanity.

This was, as we cowpersons might say, a mixed herd. Men and women both going across tonight. I didn't get an exact head count—there were just too many people wandering around in the dark for that—but I'd say there were at least sixty people, plus Braxton and me and the drivers. There were more men in the group than women, but I wouldn't hazard a guess on the ratio.

Probably because of the numbers of people and vehicles involved, the rendezvous point had been changed. Instead of meeting at the bus stop, we assembled in the unlighted parking lot of a warehouse on the outskirts of Juárez and took off in convoy from there.

I probably should have been feeling pretty good. I had no idea what all might have been said when Major Samuels spoke to Ev Robertson, but it had been enough to make the man listen to me with at least some degree of credibility after the call.

"This is contrary to my better judgment," Samuels had emphasized, "but I will give you a chance to prove yourself."

Damned decent of him, I was sure.

Still, in a way I guess it was.

He hadn't really been all that thoroughly convinced, but he had agreed to lay on an ambush and bust with his troops where we were going to cross.

With any degree of luck, Mr. Braxton would be behind bars before this night was over. It would be only a partial repayment for what had happened to Julio, I knew, but the chances seemed almighty slim that I could prove anything worse than coyoteism on the fellow at this late date.

And in spite of everything else, vigilante executions of the coldblooded kind are considerably more than I could stomach. I live with more than enough guilts, thank you, to want to add something like that to the nighttime rememberings.

So we loaded up with a maximum of confusion and a bare minimum of efficiency and headed east on a route that I did not recognize from the other crossings.

I was riding in Braxton's van as a passenger again, and I couldn't help noticing this time that he was carrying some sort of short gun in his waistband. Under the circumstances, just in case he might figure out who turned him, I was glad to have the cold bulk of the slim Browning in my pocket.

We finally reached the highway—well, sort of a highway—that I remembered and were on track toward the soon-to-be-aborted crossing.

I felt a little bad about being the instrument that would dash the hopes of so many wets.

These people were looking forward to steady jobs that would enable them to live and to eat and to help support their families back home, wherever that might be. I'm sure it made no difference at all to them that the jobs would be in the U.S. In fact, I'm sure they would have preferred to have regular work back home, where they could have gone on living with their families. The problem here was not that they despised their homeland. They just figured they had to leave it if they were to make a go of things. No matter how you cut it, it would be hard to hate a man for that.

I just hoped there was no one in the crowd from Guatemala or El Salvador or such. They say those folks are running for even better reasons than food in their kids' bellies. Some of them, I'm told, face execution if they are caught and deported back to their homes. I'd damn sure hate to have that on my conscience.

"You're quiet tonight," Braxton said to me as we rode. He had to speak up to be heard over the din of Spanish that was coming from the back of the van.

"There's a lot on the line tonight," I said.

Duke grinned. "Don't worry about it." He looked at his watch. "In another ten minutes some of my boys will be deactivating *la migra's* ears. They won't know we're around until we've been there and gone."

I raised an eyebrow. "Ears?"

"Listening devices. They don't have many along here, but there are some. We'll be walking practically over top of one tonight."

"How do you keep up with where they put them?" I was fairly sure we hadn't been in the neighborhood of any electronic snoopery the other times we had crossed. Certainly Braxton had not said anything about it those times.

And it occurred to me with a somewhat sinking feeling

that if Braxton had a pipeline of his own into the Border Patrol office, like a girlfriend or a paid informer or something, he would already know that I'd set him up for a fall. If that was so, I would be the one being set up now and not Mr. Braxton.

"Hell, they don't move them around much, Carl. I guess the locations are supposed to be secret, but they aren't. It's all routine business."

"I don't remember you saying anything about them before."

"We didn't cross by one before."

"What?"

"There isn't one on the path by the first marker, that's all." His attention was on the stretch of road illuminated by the headlights out front. He seemed perfectly at ease.

"But . . ."

"What?"

"I thought you said we were crossing at the same place. You know. Where I already know the path."

"Nah." He reached up with a forefinger and scratched his nose. "We'll be going on down a ways. No sweat, Carl. It's a good path. You don't have to worry about getting lost."

Son of a gun!

I didn't have a thing to worry about.

Right.

Major J. T. Samuels and all available hands were right this minute lying in wait at the wrong damned path. *And I was the chuckleheaded SOB who had put them there.*

I wondered whether my cell would have television and running water.

23

We went to the *fifth* rock cairn and stopped two-tenths of a mile beyond it. How many had he told me there were? I couldn't remember. Not that it made any difference. We hadn't stopped at the first one. That was what did matter.

It bothered me some that I couldn't recall exactly how many there were. I think my brain was a bit numb at the moment, thinking about those Border Patrol men waiting back there for a bunch of wets who wouldn't show.

Me they would be able to find tomorrow. By then the wets would be well on their way to Detroit or Boston or some damn place. I didn't really care about that. I did care about what Major Samuels was going to conclude when he spent a lonely night out there in the brush.

I had mighty scant expectation that he wouldn't hear about this crossing, too. El Paso/Juárez is a pretty big area but not so dang big that rumors and whisperings won't reach eager ears. I thought the good major's ears would be very keenly tuned after tonight.

Dammit!

We were in the lead of the procession of vehicles hauling all the wets. Duke pulled off onto the shoulder of the road and killed the lights, and the others rolled to a halt behind us.

It took only a few minutes for the other drivers to unload their wets and take off back the way we had come. Lucky them, I thought. Their jobs were done, and they would have nothing to worry about come the dawn.

It took a little longer for Duke to establish some degree of order in the crowd of milling, chattering Mexicans who were going to make the crossing.

He told them in a lengthy spiel of Spanish what they could expect, and then in English, an abbreviated version, I'm sure, told me, "Absolute silence tonight, Carl. It isn't as critical as it might have been, but there's no need for them to know that. We all have to stay together. No strays and no side excursions. Anyone can't keep up, leave them. You got that?"

I nodded.

"No exceptions. I don't care if it's a Vera Cruz virgin needing time to give birth, Carl, once we start moving we don't stop.

"Another thing, if we're hit by bandits, we make no fuss at all. Understood?"

I nodded again.

"I hope so. Last time you could have gotten your group in trouble. You were lucky. Tonight don't take any chances. None. If we're hit, stop and pay up and then get moving again. This is too big to ruin playing the hero."

"I understand," I assured him. At the moment I was fretting about things much more worrisome than some small-time Mexican-border bandits, although he couldn't have known that. At least I hoped he couldn't.

"I take the lead," Braxton said, "and you bring up the tail. Remember: no noise and no straggling. You remember that, and we'll all have a nice quiet walk across the river. Okay?"

"Okay."

He began to speak Spanish again, and after a little while everyone was assembled more or less into an order of march. The women were put up toward the head of the column, with the men in front of my drag position. It was not, I noticed, unlike herding cattle.

Duke started off, with the wets strung out close behind him.

There was no fence at this particular point. I don't know if there had been one or not, but at least we didn't have that to contend with. The fence I remembered off to the west, opposite where the major and his boys would be waiting, was at least a dozen miles away.

Hardly close enough, I thought, to holler, "Hey, fellas, over here." If I intended to rectify my little error, it was going to have to be some way other than that.

We were farther from the river here, too. Duke went along at his slow, steady pace for at least two miles before I became aware of some noises up ahead, and the line of wets began to accordion to a halt.

"What is it?" I asked the men who were immediately ahead of me. I should have remembered, but didn't, that they would have no idea what the hell I was asking. Or if they did guess it, they would have no way to answer me anyhow.

Bandits, I figured. It was just the kind of luck I should have expected tonight. I did some serious cussing under my breath.

And, Braxton's instructions notwithstanding, I felt of the blocky, straight grip of the Browning in my pocket.

These poor wets had enough troubles without this.

The wets looked scared, but at least they remembered to keep quiet while they were worrying. I couldn't blame them for their fears. This was one damned hazardous undertaking for them, and for all they knew, that might be *la migra* up there about to nail them one and all.

I slipped forward along the line, motioning to the wets to stay where they were and to be quiet. They seemed to look a bit less nervous as I passed. I couldn't help remembering that I was supposed to represent safety and success to them.

It seemed to take an awfully long time to pass the length of the column toward Braxton's end. Spread out in single file, this was a whole bunch of people. They hadn't seemed so darn many when they were bunched together.

As I'd expected, there were some strangers up at the front. I knew they weren't our wets because these guys were carrying handguns and giving orders.

The women, up there at the front, were the ones getting it first. One man stood off to the side with his gun on Braxton while another stood guard and a third went about the business of taking the money and any valuables from the women, one at a time.

The guy doing the searching spent a few extra moments with each woman to pat her down. The idea, I'm sure, was that he was supposed to be looking for hidden valuables. It was pretty dark, but I got the impression he was also enjoying himself.

He had already gone by a number of the women by the time I got there. Now he reached a woman, scarcely more than a girl, who was fairly attractive. I remembered noticing her before. The guy made no pretense of patting her down. He said something to her in a harsh tone of voice, and the poor gal began to strip off her clothes.

One of the other men spoke, and the guy doing the searching laughed. The wets in the line looked uncomfortable.

Whatever had been said—and it took little understanding to make a guess—the woman stopped taking off her clothes and stepped out of the line to join the bandit who was standing guard. She looked like she was resigned to a bad situation. Braxton said something to her too, but it didn't seem to cheer her up any.

Probably offering her a free crossing the next time, I guessed. Big deal. Whatever it was, it sure looked like the damn robbers intended to keep the poor gal for a while.

It pissed me off.

Braxton had told me to be a good boy, I knew, and to keep my place regardless.

Well, the hell with that.

I wasn't in his line of work, and I didn't want to be. It is one thing to try to help people. Even to make a profit from it. It is quite another to stand idly by and watch some poor damned innocent person take abuse off of a creep.

Besides, while I wasn't quite blown yet, come morning and the descent of the Border Patrol I had no future playing Duke Braxton's good buddy.

So the hell with them.

And if a little gunfire carried far enough on the still night air to bring *la migra* running, well, that would be just peachy keen too.

I pulled the Browning out of my pocket and, as silently as I could, worked the slide to jack a cartridge into the chamber.

It was pretty dark, but there was some light available. Enough to more or less see what was going on. I spread my feet to about shoulder width and squared off facing the crumb who had the woman by the arm. I felt to make sure the safety was off and used the approved two-hand hold to draw down fine just above the creep's beltline. I took a breath, let out half of it, and began the slow squeeze that would arrive directly at a let-off.

Dammit!

So I'm not big on the idea of blowing away unsuspecting bastards from ambush.

I let off on the trigger, swiveled the muzzle off to the side by a couple feet, and finished applying the trigger pressure.

Click!

Or maybe it was more of a *clunk*.

Whatever, it was a dry snap of the internal hammer dropping onto nothing of much interest.

The damn gun didn't fire.

A dud? That seemed fairly incredible in this day of surefire ammo.

Still, no one seemed to have heard the soft tap of metal on metal, so I tried it again. Jacked another round into place, made sure everything was as it was supposed to be, and squeezed off another drop of the hammer, this time with the muzzle pointed kind of upward.

The only result was a repeat of that thin, dry snap.

Nothing.

Either I had been given a deliberately sabotaged gun or the damned Browning was busted. I was going to be darn well interested in knowing which, but not at the moment. As far as that woman over there would care, it mattered not at all. I shoved the Browning back into my pocket, scowled quite a lot, and soft-footed it back the way I had come, back to my proper place at the end of the column of wets. The guy who was doing the robbing and searching was still at work and moving faster now that he was frisking men instead of petrified women. I didn't want him to reach the end of the line and find anything out-of-place.

On the other hand, I wasn't quite ready yet to forget about the woman who had been yanked out of the line.

24

The guy completed his appointed task. By that time the sack he was carrying had a distinct bulge from all the goodies, primarily paper goodies, that had been chucked into it.

I noticed that he ignored me completely. I was standing beside the last man in line, but the robber never so much as glanced in my direction. He did his thing with the defenseless wets and pretended that Coyote Carl was nowhere around.

The robber cupped a hand to his mouth and made a sound that I believe was supposed to be some kind of birdcall. Either it was an excellent imitation of a bird I've never heard before or it was a truly lousy birdcall. Whatever, the line began to shuffle forward a minute or so later, and the happy bandit faded off to the side.

That particular creep was my only point of reference for finding the others, so as soon as I thought it was safe I detached myself from the line and Injuned back to him.

The man stood there until the column of wets was out of sight, then he walked briskly forward and off to one side from the path.

He obviously wasn't thinking in terms of being followed and was making no attempt to walk quietly, so I didn't even have to use any grade-A efforts to stay with him. I just ghosted along behind him with my eyes and ears open.

Hell-lo, I thought.

The guy joined three other men and the woman after a short walk north. I'd thought there were three men, but there were four. Possibly it was just as well that the lousy Browning hadn't fired then.

The men were in cheerful conversation. I wished I could understand what they were saying, but I couldn't. The slumped set of the woman's shoulders indicated that she might be feeling just a bit less cheerful than the men.

The creeps didn't seem to be in any huge rush to jump her bones, I noticed. That was good. I wouldn't have to feel compelled to do the wrong thing rapidly. I dropped down to the deck and reminded myself to pretend this country wasn't thorny. I tried to make like a snake and slithered forward slow and easy.

The bandits themselves were making it somewhat simpler. They were still talking, and two of them were rummaging through the loot in their bag.

"All *right,*" one of them said happily.

I froze.

That voice was damn well recognizable.

It seemed that the good Mr. Braxton was still on the scene.

He was the fourth man. The creep I'd thought I had missed spotting before.

Jesus.

He must have given the wets instructions to go on ahead along the path and wait for him there. Like at the river. That would be logical.

But the woman. Dammit, she certainly had recognized

him by now as part of the robbery. The son of a bitch was standing right there taking a cut.

That was not entirely the sort of information Mr. Braxton would want to have floating around on the streets of Juárez. El coyote, the friendly gringo chap who not only charges you a fee for his services, he also strips you of everything you own.

No, I didn't really think he wanted potential customers to know that.

And he had promised the gal another attempt—or at least I assumed that was what he had told her—that now looked to be a mighty false ray of hope.

As far as I could see, the only way Braxton could preserve his sterling reputation now would be to let his robber chums use the woman and then throw her away. A disposable human being. Discard after use.

Obviously the son of a bitch had been willing to trust his pals for a split on the routine jobs, but this one was larger. He wanted to take his cut on the spot to make sure he got all of his share.

If that meant that a person had to die to protect his interests, well, after all she was just another wet. There were lots of those around.

Julio's life hadn't been worth a hassle. This gal's wouldn't be either. They were both just a couple lousy wetbacks.

Son of a *bitch!*

Braxton took a wad of money, folded it neatly, and tucked it into a pocket of the dark blue windbreaker he was wearing. He said goodbye to his pals and hurried off into the night to meet the column of wets.

Those poor folks were at the moment wandering through the night without any guidance. Although they wouldn't know that. Braxton thought I was still with them. And the people at the back of the line would think Braxton was still with them. I shook my head. If anybody knew all that was going on with this fouled-up crossing, they'd *all* be panicked.

Still, Braxton's absence made things easier for me, and I was glad he was going back to his duties elsewhere. I suspected he could be a rough one to handle, and I sure didn't want to tangle with him when he had help.

I waited until he was out of sight, then snaked forward again.

I probably could have fired up a cigarette and tromped up there with my hands in my pockets. The creeps had their attention solely on the girl and weren't thinking at all about watching their backsides.

This, I thought, was going to be a pleasure.

25

"Good evening, Carl. Lost?"

I cussed a little.

Braxton was there waiting for me. The crowd of wets was huddled in the brush beyond him.

I guess he had come up to the rear of the column and discovered that I wasn't where I was supposed to be. Maybe he figured out what I was up to. Certainly he would have been afraid about what I might have seen back there.

Well, he had good enough reason. I'd seen more than enough.

And it was obvious, too, from what I was carrying that I'd found his buddy bandits. I had their loot sack in my hand. The idea was to return it to the owners.

Braxton, I gathered, might have another notion about that. He did not look or sound very friendly now.

It would have been real useful if I could have done some loud talking, loud enough for the wets to hear. Unfortunately, I could have yammered the rest of the night away, and they wouldn't have been able to understand a bit of it.

The girl would have helped too. If she had come with me, she could have told them what was up.

As it was, as soon as she got loose from the son of a bitch who'd had hold of her she had taken off lickety-split for points south.

I knew good and well she'd seen me there, plenty close enough to see who I was. But she had no way to know that I was there trying to help her. Hell, she'd just seen the head coyote turn her over to the bandits. As far as she would know, I was just wanting to get in line with the others. So I didn't blame the kid for taking off like that. At the moment her presence sure would have been useful, though. Pity.

"You didn't answer me, Carl."

"No, I guess I didn't."

"No denials?"

I shrugged. "Why bother?"

"Why indeed." Duke sighed. "It isn't nice to be greedy, Carl. You could have had a good thing going here, but you had to get greedy and get in the way of a nice operation."

"Greedy? Oh. This." I hefted the bag.

"Uh-huh, that."

I grinned at him. "Perhaps you fail to fully understand the situation, my man."

"Oh, I think I understand well enough."

"Do you remember a kid named Julio, Duke?"

The light was poor, but I thought he looked puzzled. "I've known boys named Julio by the hundreds. Why?"

"This one was a kid from down south. Julio Cervantes. He paid you to bring him across one night. He never made it to the other side, and he never made it back south either."

Braxton shrugged. "Who remembers? Something happens, the Mexes all split, who the hell knows what might happen to them afterward. I can't be responsible for all of them, man. You ought to know that. Besides, what do you care? It's no fat off your ox."

"Fact is, Duke, it is my affair." I smiled at him. "I was hired to come down here and take it real personal about Julio."

"Shit. Private detective, that sort of thing?"

"More like a favor for a friend. My kind of thing—I don't want the paperwork that'd go with the formalities of being a detective. Much more private than that." I was edging slightly forward as I talked. Shifting my feet back and forth and managing to get just a hair closer each time.

"Hired muscle, Carl? Come on. You didn't really come down here to off me, did you?"

I grinned at him. The guy was carrying a gun, after all. If I could get him a little bit nervous, it might be useful.

"What happened to the, uh, others?" He was looking at that bag in my hand. It would not take actual genius to figure out that those banditos had not handed it over just because I said please.

I shrugged. "They're all three back there," I said. "Somewhere."

That was true enough. I'm sure they still were, somewhere. The last I'd seen them they were limping and gimping along in a generally southerly direction. I doubt that they felt very well, but they were still alive. I didn't feel honor-bound to tell Braxton that.

"You do want . . ."

The talk was just so much cover-up, trying to take my attention off what he was doing and put it onto what he was saying.

His hand moved, and he snatched at the gun behind his belt.

I whapped him with the bag of money. Kinda like a little old lady swatting a mugger with her purse.

The burlap connected with the automatic Braxton was pulling, and the thing went flying.

Christians 1, Lions 0.

Braxton—darn it—was not willing to holler Uncle and let me do with him as I wished. And in spite of his size he was not exactly either slow or weak.

He didn't try to get away. I guess no matter how strong a man is, if he is carrying a lot of weight, even all of it muscle, he can't depend on foot speed when it comes to personal-safety time.

Instead of running, he came at me. Fast.

I wanted no part of a rough-and-tumble tussle with this guy, so I let go of the dead weight of the burlap sack and ducked off to the side.

Damn, Braxton was quick.

Most guys, you slip aside like that and they'll go roaring right on past like a coal train on a downgrade. Not this one.

He made his adjustment in mid-lunge and slammed a fist into me with, thank goodness, a glancing blow. If I'd been standing still, the scrap would have been all over right there and then. If the punch had landed just a little cleaner I would have had a broken rib at the very least. As it was I hurt like hell.

I made it a point to dance away from that man, but pronto.

"Bastard," he screamed. "Prick." He was barely beginning to get warmed up. Apparently he liked to shout a lot when he was fighting. Called me some rather offensive things, he did.

He took another lunge at me, but it was a feint. He'd hardly gotten well started in my direction when he did some fast and fancy footwork and launched a boot toe toward where my crotch would have been if I'd darted to the left again. Considering what he was calling me, though, I really hadn't expected that we would play by the Queensberry rules.

I made a flat fist with the knuckles forward and slugged him just below the point of the shoulder, which was about all that I thought was safe to reach for the moment. I didn't expect any immediate reaction and didn't get one, but I knew good and well that he didn't have as much use of that arm as he had a moment or two earlier.

Still shouting and cursing, he whirled and tried another kick for the groin. Definitely not friendly behavior.

I sidestepped and nailed him another one just below the point of the other shoulder.

"Bastard," he yelled again. Actually by now he was getting kinda repetitious about the name-calling. Limited imagination, I figured.

Braxton came leaping toward me again. Again I moved quickly to dodge the expected kick.

Unfortunately he wasn't kicking this time. And his arms weren't so well damaged that he couldn't throw a helluva punch. A straight left came in on me like a bale of wet timothy dropped square on my jaw.

There was power behind it but less snap than there might have been, and I was able to roll with it. That helped, I'm sure, but it was still plenty painful. I could feel a trickle of something warm and wet going down my neck.

He tried a kick again, but this time it was my turn. I punched him *under* the jaw, square on the Adam's apple, and was rewarded with a rather ugly sound of gagging and hoarse straining for air.

While Braxton was preoccupied with the necessity of breathing, I went to work again trying to paralyze his arm muscles.

The son of a bitch was built like a bull, though, and he was not interested in quitting. He whirled and flailed, and as far as I could tell I really hadn't done him much damage yet. Entirely too little damage, in fact.

And if he ever caught me one good one, well, I didn't know if I could come back from it or not.

So much for fighting more or less fair. I really did *not* want this mad SOB to get his hands on me.

I stepped back and pretended to stagger, inviting another of the uplifting Braxton kicks to the cods.

Sure enough, he delivered it.

Instead of dodging to the side this time, though, I stepped inside the swing of his boot and gave him a kick of his own to think about. I caught him on the kneecap damn near hard enough to fell a blue spruce. I heard something that might have been cartilage popping, and Braxton went down screaming.

He lay doubled over on the ground, shrieking curses, and I took a moment to recapture some lost breath.

Braxton was lying there curled up into a tight ball with

his hands clutched to his belly. I was bent over gulping down the wind.

Just in time I remembered that it was the damned man's leg that was supposed to be hurt here, not his gut.

I stepped out of the way in time to watch with some interest while a steel blade flashed in an arc right where my ankle had been a half-moment before.

"Very naughty, Duke," I said.

"Bastard."

"You've mentioned that before."

Like I said, I was not willing to play games or take chances with a guy as quick and as tough as this one. And if he wanted to make a knife fight of it now, well, it was a game I didn't want to play.

He was on the ground. To come at me he would have to get up. When he tried it, I was ready for him. I stepped into him with a knee lifted smartly into his face and took advantage of the moment to relieve him of the switchblade in his fist.

Taking no chances, I also dropped low to get the leverage I wanted, yanked back with this hand, and shoved hard forward with that one. Braxton's elbow reached the end of its travel and went somewhat past it. The sound of the joint letting go was quite distinct, if ugly as hell.

Braxton screamed.

Still the son of a bitch wouldn't quit.

He got his other hand into my hair and pulled, and I went over sideways.

Thank goodness for small favors like broken arms. If it hadn't been for that, I'd have been a dead man.

He still had hold of my hair with his one good hand. I rolled my head to the side, got his thumb into my mouth, and clamped down hard enough to bring blood and tear flesh. He let go, and I rolled away.

I'd told myself long before then to ignore such petty annoyances as cactus spines, but I guess I needed a reminder. A patch of undersized cacti reminded me.

"Dammit, Duke, leave off now or I'll have to break the other arm."

His answer was to grab up the knife that had been dropped and throw it at me.

My luck was running high for a change. It hit flat instead of point first and didn't do any more damage than to put a hole in my shirt.

"I told you not to do that, Duke." I bent and picked up the knife. I will admit that I was feeling as winded and shot as if I'd just made that assinine annual marathon run up Pikes Peak.

I figured Braxton was done for now too. I kicked around and found the pistol he had dropped and shoved it into my left-hand pants pocket—the right pocket was still occupied by the useless Browning.

I turned and tried to think of some way to explain to the confused wetbacks just what in hell had been going on here between their two trusted coyotes. I needn't have bothered. There wasn't another soul in sight. They had every one of them rabbited during our little scrap.

Damn, I thought.

I turned, intending to get Braxton up and moving toward the border and the mercies of Major Samuels.

The son of a bitch was on his feet and coming for me.

I didn't think about it. My hand came up to try to fend him off, and the point of his own blade slid neatly between his ribs.

It was, I think, about as close to accidental death as a person could come in the midst of a serious fight.

Braxton grunted and went down.

I was left standing there in the light of a rising sliver of moon with a dead man, assorted weaponry, and quite a lot of stolen money.

It had been, I thought, one damned long night already.

26

I didn't leave that spot right away. It may seem a little macabre for me to have been sitting there in the night beside the empty husk that had been Duke Braxton, but for a while there my knees were not being especially cooperative. Particularly after I got done picking the man's pockets for the keys to his van and the several wads of cash he had on him. One of those would have been the share of the loot he had gotten from the bandits. The rest, I suppose, was the even larger wad he had taken as fees from the now-departed wets.

Those folks sure hadn't gotten what they had bargained for on this night.

When I felt up to it, all the various working parts of me, I got up and walked on north, the way we had been going.

There was still a mess of trucks and drivers over there, and I was having some fanciful ideas about them.

You know the sort of thing. Bugles blowing and guidons flapping. Charge in on the white horse. Gather up all the guys in the black hats and turn them over to Marshal/Major Samuels.

Shucks, with any luck at all Samuels's primary sidekick in the green suit would have a stiff right leg and be called Chester.

Oh well. A fella can't have everything.

I was already practically on the riverbank, and the path picked up just the other side of it. I had no trouble following it even though I'd not been on it before.

There were only two trucks waiting over there to pick up the wets that were supposed to have crossed, but both of them were wingdingers for size. They were tractor-trailer rigs, painted like, stolen from, or maybe rented from Mayflower, the moving-van outfit. If I had to guess, I would say that they'd been painted to look like the real thing, because an outfit with that kind of reputation wouldn't stoop to transporting illegal aliens, I wouldn't think, and no one moving van driver on the road would know all the other drivers who were legitimately flying the same colors.

Anyway, they were no trick at all to spot, and I walked up to them and howdied from a few rods out.

The hello got a reaction too. A pair of men—Anglos all—tumbled out of each cab on the double quick with guns in their hands.

"Hold it," I said plenty loud enough to be heard. "Duke sent me."

"Where're the others?" one of them asked.

"Back there." I hooked a thumb over my shoulder in the general direction of the river. "They'll be along in a few minutes."

Personally, I thought it was a good and logical way to get up close to them, where I might have some sort of edge with

Braxton's gun and my own useless Browning to cover them with.

Wrong.

Apparently Braxton had thought to give them some sort of password or procedure for unusual contingencies, because they sure didn't act friendly.

The first I knew something was wrong was when the idjits began shooting.

Have you ever seen the kind of yellow halo and spear of flame a pistol makes at night when it's pointed at you? It is not one of life's more attractive views.

I flopped down right *now*. Picked up some more stickers in doing so but didn't mind a single one of them this time. They were much more comfortable than a bullet would have been.

Braxton's drivers, thank goodness, didn't hang around trying to make sure they got me. They probably thought I was just the first of a bunch of greens anyhow.

They let off one fast, furious fusillade and beat it for their trucks.

It was kind of interesting to see just how fast a man can scale the heights of a Kenworth's sides. It was much quicker than I would have believed.

The engines fired up at the first spin, and those empty trailers were leaping and bucking over the ruts in jig time.

I got back up and dusted myself off. That's when I discovered all the fresh cactus spines, so I plucked at them while I walked back south the way I had come.

Braxton's van was back in that direction a ways, and I was going to need transportation back to Juárez.

I was also, I realized, going to need to think of some tall tale to spin for Samuels and his boys. I doubted that the man was going to be real happy with me the next time we met.

27

There are a few rare and wonderful moments in life when you don't even have to lie to stay out of jail. My visit with Major Samuels the next morning was one of them.

I had gone there of my own free will—much more dignified, I thought, than being dragged in by bodily force—and darned if the man wasn't reasonably agreeable.

"I've already heard," Samuels said after an almost informal greeting. "We picked up some of the illegals on the highway trying to make it into the interior on their own. They told us there was some sort of fracas after the bandits hit them. Pity about those bandits, you know, Heller. I would really like to do something about them, but of course we are not allowed to operate in any capacity on the other side of the border." He shook his head.

Then he actually smiled. Not one of those thin-lipped jobs like I was the sparrow and he was the feline, but the genuine article. It was the first such expression I'd seen out of the man. "You did try though, Heller. We appreciate cooperative assistance from the general public. We truly do."

I suppose I should have smiled nice and smugly and kept my mouth shut and gone quietly away, but I guess I'm just not built with that kind of good sense—or lack of curiosity.

"Any word on what might have happened to Braxton, Major?"

"Nothing. We will be watching him, of course, when he does surface again. I shouldn't imagine it would be long. The man has more than his share of cheek, you know."

"He told me you believe he's just another local who goes across to play with the girlies."

Samuels smiled again. "Is that the cover he was trying to establish? I never knew that."

So much for the cleverness of petty crooks. I stood and shook the major's hand. "Sorry this didn't work out better for you, sir."

"You tried, Mr. Heller, and we are grateful. If I could offer a word of advice?"

"Please."

"Further involvement with these coyotes could be dangerous for you. I suggest you stay away from them in future." The slightly British phrasing there seemed, oddly, to be quite in character for this stiff-necked fellow. It seemed to fit. And I was willing to bet that he would be pure hell in a gunfight.

"I'll take that advice, sir. I have a few more things to do down here, but believe me it's going to be a pleasure to get home again."

Believe me, I felt better walking out of there than I had going in. And the odds were that when the major finally heard about Braxton he would think, and so would the Mexican authorities, that it was the bandits who had knifed him.

I headed back to the hotel and to Leah, who was also under a selected few misconceptions about what all had happened the night before.

I needed to make a few calls from there. One to Carmen.

I figured she would be the best choice for leaving the money with in the hope that some of it might be returned to the owners. Some of it, anyhow. I was kind of appropriating Braxton's share, all in dollars, for other purposes. And I needed to call Raoul. I wanted to see him one more time before we left, too.

In the meantime, I was looking forward to giving Leah some of the careful attention that she deserved.

28

Raoul met me at La Florida. He still reminded me of a politician. This evening he was wearing a beautifully tailored navy-blue suit, with vest of course, that had pinstripes of a silvery gray hue that almost exactly matched the silver gray at his temples. His tie was knotted so precisely that I had to wonder if he employed a valet to help with such details. As far as I know, I've never met a man before who had a valet, and I decided not to ask Raoul about it; I didn't want to spoil the illusion just in case he didn't have one.

"It is a great pleasure, Carl," he said, "and I congratulate you on achieving your, uh, purpose here."

"Thanks. You've heard then."

"About Señor Braxton? Yes. Regrettable, I suppose, or it should be. Of course we Latinos," he smiled, "have long traditions of revenge. We understand the necessity for vengeance, you see."

I smiled back at him. "I've heard that. In fact, I wanted to talk to you about it."

"Really? About what?"

"Later. After the meal."

"Of course. An appreciation of cuisine is also appreciated here."

Both the service and the food were, as before, just terrific. Raoul had quail stuffed with wild rice, and I had a rare steak that was fork-cutting tender. Raoul insisted that we each have a bottle of wine of our own, a white for him and a red for me. I'm sure they were terrific too. Certainly he had a helluva fun time with the wine steward deciding on them. I *think* they were speaking English, out of courtesy to the crass foreigner, but it might have been some brand-new language for all I understood of it. And I'll bet if I had the kind of educated palate that lets you tell such things, instead of my plain old preference for Coors or homemade sour mash white whiskey, why, I'd really have enjoyed the French stuff that was finally delivered. As it was I didn't think it was awful.

Anyway, we dined—didn't eat, mind, we dined—in great comfort and polished it off with a dessert of fresh mango on a bed of shaved ice.

Oh, it was dandy.

Later, over coffee and brandy—cigars were offered too, which Raoul accepted while I stuck with my cigarettes—Raoul said, "There was something you wanted to discuss with me, my friend?"

"Uh-huh." I took my time about getting some ash off the tip of my smoke. "For one thing, Raoul, I wanted to return the pistol you got for me."

"It was nothing, my friend."

"True."

"Eh?"

I smiled. "I agree. It was nothing. No firing pin."

"No?" His eyes widened. "But you could have been injured, Carl. Accept my apologies, please. I must speak with the friend who provided it." He went on in that vein for some time, and I waited him out.

"Well, it worked out okay anyhow," I said finally. I bent closer to the table and pulled the Browning out from under my shirt and handed it to him under the table. It disappeared with a magician's touch. "You might want to have that thing fixed," I said.

"I shall."

"You might need it, Raoul."

He smiled and shook his head. "Not I, my friend."

"Oh, I think you might."

"So?" He looked like he really did not know what I meant.

"Uh-huh." I was smiling. "You said yourself, my man, Latinos have this thing about revenge. It's a point of honor, and honor is very big down here, the way I understand it."

"But I do not understand you, Carl."

"Oh, I reckon you do, Raoul. Though it took me a while to work it out." I grinned. "You thought you couldn't lose, didn't you?"

"Lose?"

"Sure. Carmen told you there was this damn Yankee from Colorado coming down to get vengeance for poor ol' Julio, and you offered all the help you could. You had to figure you couldn't lose. If Duke offed me, the threat was done with. And if I got Duke, that was a different thorn out of your side.

"What was Braxton doing, Raoul? Was he getting too greedy? Setting up more and more on his own? Taking too big a cut out of the robberies in addition to the fees?"

"I do not know—"

"Of course you do, my man. Course you do."

Raoul looked a little more numb than confused now, and he had quit trying to sputter out denials.

"Actually, it was the major over at the Border Patrol who told me what was going on. Not that he knew it. But he'd said something to me about me being seen with a known trafficker in illegals, Raoul. I figured at the time he was talking about Braxton, but he wasn't, was he?"

"Of course he—"

"No, because the Border Patrol isn't allowed to do anything on the Juárez side of the border, Raoul. They never come over here. They don't have any surveillance on this side. Just on the U.S. side of the line. I never talked to Duke over there. We always met in some joint or restaurant here in Juárez. Never in El Paso.

"You, though, we ate with over there several times. Did you know the Patrol is onto you, Raoul? They are. They keep an eye on you every time you're on their side of the border. I confirmed that with Samuels this afternoon. After all the odd little cogs started to mesh and I began to realize that Braxton couldn't have been the one they saw me with. But you, sure, they saw me talking with you, and I hadn't admitted a thing to them about meeting with a coyote named Raoul. That's one of the things that made them so suspicious about me to begin with.

"Of course I'm probably slighting you when I call you a coyote, aren't I? Sure. You're no hired hand to go slinking around in the night. You'd get your shoes dirty and everything. Couldn't have that for a man in your position, could you? But you could hire guys to do that part of it. You, Raoul, you're above that. You just set up the poor sons of bitches who are going to pay heavy to be taken across, and you set up the crumbs who are going to rob them of everything else they have. And more than likely you set up the sales of those poor bastards to employers, too. I don't know that, of course. It's just a guess. Braxton didn't seem like the kind to have the contacts that would take, so I think it's a logical guess." I smiled again. "Not that I give a crap myself. It doesn't really matter."

"But . . ."

"Hell, Raoul, I'm not even going to tell the Border Patrol what I'm guessing. Or maybe I will. I haven't really decided that yet. In the long run I don't think it will matter very much what they know or don't know, because you won't be around very long, Raoul. You won't be around very long at all."

Raoul's eyes narrowed, and now he didn't look at all like the distinguished, dignified politician. "You are threatening me, Carl?"

"Me? Hell no, Raoul. Not me. I'm done down here. Braxton is dead. Which seems fitting. You know, gringo against gringo and all that. So that part of it worked out okay. Now I figure to let Julio's family have the rest of the pleasure. I've already given them your name, Raoul, and there are plenty of pictures of you available. Carmen checked that for me. She says you've been very busy down here with the civic-minded things. You've had lots of pictures taken while you donated to this or helped out with that. So all the Cervantes boys will know who they are looking for.

"Hell, Raoul, you even provided them with travel expenses to come looking for you. Did you know that? It's true. Braxton was carrying it last night, but I reckon a lot of it could be considered yours. Julio's brothers and his cousins have it now. They're going to use it to help hunt you down, Raoul. I'm told they're looking forward to the chase." I sat back and lit another cigarette. "The family promises they'll let me know how long it takes, Raoul. With any luck there will be enough money left over to set up a real nice mass for Julio. So if you want to do the decent thing, Raoul, you won't run from them too hard. Give them a break, huh? They're nice folks."

Raoul hissed something at me that it was probably just as well for me not to understand.

He reached under his coat but then seemed to remember in time that the damned Browning didn't work. I smiled at him.

"Go ahead, Raoul. I'll understand if you want to leave now. I won't be offended. And don't worry about the check. It's my treat this time."

He was kind of pale when he hurried out of the restaurant.

And he was already learning to look over his shoulder when he reached a public street.

I wondered if all that stuff about Latins and revenge was true. I was sure willing to believe that Raoul thought it was. I took my time about finishing my smoke and my brandy before I paid the check and took a taxi back across to my own side of the border.

29

It took us three days to get back home in Leah's soft-sprung Cadillac. Even with that cloudlike suspension the pain was getting awfully bad for her. She had been away from doctoring just too long, I think, although she kept denying it. It was to a regular M.D. in El Paso that she had disappeared that one afternoon, and I guess that had been too little. Or maybe it was simply too late.

Or in another way not too late at all.

We had seven weeks together after we got home, and I was grateful for each and every one of them.

They tried to talk her into going to a hospice in Pueblo for the last month, but Leah wouldn't go. She said she didn't need to. She had Stella and she had me, and she told them that was enough.

And at least they didn't try to talk her into any last-minute desperation attempts with the knife or radiation or whatever. They just prescribed all the relief that was medically available for her and let her have the kind of happiness that she wanted.

She made Stella and me both promise that we wouldn't cry for her.

We made the promise, but it was one neither of us could keep.

I still miss her.

But I don't have any regrets about her. Not one. She was so pleased that we were together that I have to be too, and I guess I always will be. That was just one of the very special gifts she gave me.

But, Lord, I do miss her.

ABOUT FRANK RODERUS

Like so many of my generation, and just like the song says, "my heroes have always been cowboys." I have a deep and abiding love for the American West, what it taught us, and what it stands for. But not until I moved into the high country, far from grocery stores and modern services, did I realize how very much alive the spirit of the West truly is.

Carl Heller is a product of imagination. But he could as easily be friend and neighbor.

Here where addresses are given in terms of direction from ranches and valleys, creeks and mountain peaks, the people are independent of spirit and free to rise or fall on the basis of the strengths God has granted them. Carl Heller is, quite simply, one of them.

The situations he finds himself in are taken from the newspaper headlines of today and of tomorrow. They are a part of the daily fabric of the modern West. Some of them have already happened; all of them could happen.

And like any good friend, Carl and I share many interests, many loves. We both appreciate the feel of a strong-running motorcycle swooping the curves of Ute Pass or Florissant Canyon. We both are enamored of the American Quarter Horse with its great heart and quick feet. We both dote on the brisk, clean air and the magnificent vistas of the West. In one respect I have been more fortunate than Carl, because I have a family with whom I can share these pleasures. Carl, though, is basically a friend and neighbor with whom I would be glad to share my hunting camp.